THE PRIVATE WORLD OF LEONARD BERNSTEIN

TEXT BY JOHN GRUEN

THE PRIVATE WORLD O

 A RIDGE PRESS BOOK

PHOTOGRAPHS BY KEN HEYMAN

LEONARD BERNSTEIN

WEIDENFELD AND NICOLSON/LONDON

1. How to be objective about Leonard Bernstein? The force of his personality is such that there is no neutral territory. What is more, he elicits as many contradictions and collisions of feelings as exist in him.

With Lenny everything is personal. A sense of the personal exudes from him as a force. There is no liking or disliking this. Whether it produces love or hate is irrelevant. It *is*. In trying to analyze my own feelings about him, I discover that the power and drive of his personality affect me deeply, and I find that to extricate myself from its pull is very difficult. For one thing, he elicits tremendous feelings of voluntary loyalty. For another, he has been so open with me that I feel protective of him. Unnecessarily so; his openness is his own best protection.

He and I spent seven weeks together in Italy in the summer of 1967. There was no program, no schedule. I had no idea to what extent he would give of his time. This was, after all, his vacation, and, moreover, the first vacation he and his family had ever spent abroad.

Yet, from early July to the end of August, Leonard Bernstein gave me entry to his private world. From the very first he wondered what kind of book this would be. He insisted that it not be a full-scale biography; it was not yet time for one. But he knew it would deal with his life away from the public eye. It would be about Leonard Bernstein, the man, the husband, the father, the son, the brother—his personal world as I was given to see it. It might also be a book in which he could reflect on his life as a musician and upon the world in which he lives.

But it would be more than he expected. It would be an inward journey of self-revelation —a confessional, if you will. I wanted Lenny to go deep into his feelings, deep into his life, hoping thereby to tap the roots of his emo-tional, intellectual, and musical make-up— wanting to find the components, the motors that shaped and guided his personality. He called the project hopeless, of course. As for confessionals, our very first talk began with Bernstein saying:

"Picasso's private world made a perfectly wonderful book because Picasso lives absolutely openly. He lives in a bikini in the south of France; his morality is absolutely free. I myself have a much more bourgeois background. After all, I'm the son of a rather puritanical, Mosaic-oriented Talmudic scholar. And as free as I have been, especially in my youthful years, I have never been able to escape from that strong puritan morality which comes to me both by way of the Talmudic father and the New England I grew up in, which make a very puritanical combination indeed.

"Although you may spend your youth fighting your environmental morality, protesting it, and showing what a rebel you are, it stays with you—even through some abortive attempts at psychoanalysis. I still have this bourgeois streak and I will always have it. It's a streak which is reinforced by my need to protect people I love. So there's a limit to how much I can reveal myself."

The Italian setting was a rented villa in Ansedonia, a small Roman town which, together with Porto Ercole and Porto Santo Stefano, has lately become a fashionable and expensive summer retreat for the rich, the titled, the famous, and the beautiful.

These small towns—fishing villages, really— nestle at the foot of Monte Argentario, the region's highest mountain, and lie, quite photogenically, upon the calm shores of the extremely blue Tyrrhenian Sea. Despite reports of the region's incomparable beauty, purity, and antiquity, these small towns are not among the breathtaking jewels of Italy. The Costa d'Argento was heavily bombed during World War II, and most of the architecture, apart from the sixteenth-century Spanish forts and some Roman ruins, still smells of newly poured cement. The area is being rapidly barnacled with villas: Ansedonia is well-nigh completely encrusted, while Porto Ercole and Porto Santo Stefano have been hit by the condominium complex. The co-ops keep rising, one after the other, in what promises to be dreary succession. Luckily, Monte Argentario is grand enough to dominate all of this with its moody, impassive indifference.

While the lower reaches of the mountain are heavily infested with villas owned or rented by the jet set and others, the upper two-thirds remain, as they have for centuries, firmly in the hands of the Corsinis, the Borgheses, and other Italian nobility. Here peasants continue to live and work as their fathers and grandfathers did on the same land for the same noble families. The feudal life continues.

But down below, port life is a confusing melee of activity, where cars and people thread their way along a stone quay lined with seasonal boutiques, boat houses, gas pumps, ice-cream parlors, restaurants, and small bars. The scene is all this, plus stray cats and chickens.

Moored along the quay are beat-up dinghies, sleek, bright motor launches, jostling sailboats, and gray or orange inflated rubber boats. Farther out may be seen elegant and gleaming schooners, and the mysterious white yachts of Niarchos and God knows who else. It's all excruciatingly picturesque, and as the light of day changes the setting is more Dufy than Dufy.

Of the miles of beach the less said the better. The ocean deposits upon the strand endless quantities of what appears to be horse manure, actually a low and odorless form of marine life. Unless swept clean by hotel owners or private attendants, however, the beaches of the Costa d'Argento do not invite sybaritic lolling.

The real assets are the sun, the air, and the extremely blue and buoyant sea. It is silken, calm, and transparent, and to swim in these waters, to dive for sea urchins or starfish or coral, or to explore the inner reaches of countless grottos, to spearfish or skin dive—these are the true pleasures of the area.

Out at sea, on a sailboat, one feels suspended between light and soundlessness. One is barely conscious of movement. Everything is very still, very luminous. But once on shore, villa-hopping is the order of the day and night. The usual drinks, dinner parties, and outings to restaurants (most of them remarkably mediocre) constitute the social life. At night one or two new nightclubs offer predictable discotheque refuge from the silence of nature.

The Bernstein villa, with its orchards, quiet gardens, its pool and immediate access to the sea, was not the scene of madcap social gatherings. Lenny and Felicia Bernstein were guardedly not part of the fashionable set. Invitations were seldom accepted or, indeed, extended. For them the villa was a retreat—a pretty place near the sea where the family could swim, lie in the sun, paint, read, and simply be together. And the summer in Ansedonia would be a new experience; every other summer they had gone either to the Berkshires, to Martha's Vineyard, or to their country house in Connecticut. Lenny's younger brother Burton, his wife Ellen, and their two small children Karen and Michael were also spending the summer in Italy—in nearby Porto Ercole. And they were frequent visitors.

It was agreed I would be part of this summer life. My wife Jane, my eight-year-old daughter Julia, our long-haired dachshund Sophie, and I rented a villa not far from the Bernsteins. Also on hand was photographer Ken Heyman, whose task, like mine, was to observe the many dimensions of Leonard Bernstein's world.

Lenny was the last of his family to arrive in Ansedonia. His vacation was delayed by ten days so that he might conduct the Israel Philharmonic on Mount Scopus in Jerusalem, the six-day war having been won and Bernstein having been among the first to be invited to join in a great musical celebration of the triumph.

At last, he arrived. He was both exalted and exhausted—exalted because the experience of conducting in Israel on such an occasion moved him deeply, exhausted because yet another New York Philharmonic season had recently ended. His back was giving him great trouble—a problem of long standing—and this summer the pain was to be particularly debilitating. He looked pale and drawn. In two months' time—on August 25—Bernstein would be forty-nine. The boy wonder, the young multitalented genius was definitely growing older. Still, as always, the handsome, leonine head was impressive and his presence all-pervasive.

While the object of the summer was rest and leisure, Lenny was full of projects. First and foremost, he wished to compose. He feels he has not yet begun to do so. "I have not even scratched the surface," he kept saying. Now he would make a start, a serious start. He also would begin thinking about his commission to write an opening work, an opera, for the John F. Kennedy Center being erected in Washington, D.C. A new theater piece was churning, and there was Strauss' *Der Rosenkavalier* to think about; he would conduct it in the spring at the Vienna Opera.

But from the first day, Lenny felt oppressed. Something weighed him down. He was depressed and he was restless. He quite obviously needed to relax and to unwind. All around him now were people and things that might buoy his spirits. And there was the sea, which he loves. To submerge himself in water, to be weightless and at one with its forces, produces feelings of supreme contentment in him. When he emerges from the sea he seems resuscitated both physically and spiritually.

The days passed and slowly Lenny unwound. His face and body became bronzed. Two or three times a day, he plunged into the sea or into the pool. He went sailing or took trips in a motor boat, or took long drives in his newly acquired Maserati. He did these things with Felicia and their children—fifteen-year-old Jamie, twelve-year-old Alexander, and five-year-old Nina. And Jane, Julia, and I were, more often than not, part of these activities. Life in Ansedonia settled into itself, and soon Lenny and I were able to talk.

Ansedonia, 1967: With Jamie, Nina, Alexander, Felicia

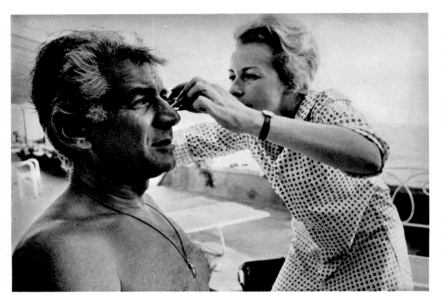

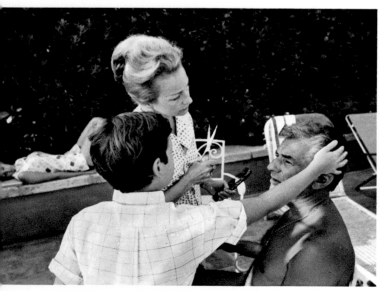

2. Dinnertime. The servants serve pasta, then fish. The wine is Italian, and good. Chatter about the heat, about the cicadas which chirp incessantly during the day and rob everyone of their nap. Jamie is reading Faulkner's *The Sound and the Fury*—the first of many books she must read during the summer for school. She says she finds it totally engrossing. Alexander, who will have his bar mitzvah the following year, hashed his first Hebrew lesson with Lenny (another of Lenny's summer projects). Lenny and Alexander have a short recap of the lesson. Felicia looks beautiful in a cool cotton dress. Earlier I had asked her to play the piano, which she did. Now she talks about how badly she played (although she had studied with Claudio Arrau in Chile, where she grew up and lived for years) and how she had wanted to become a concert pianist, but gave it up to become an actress instead. Of how she did become an actress with many roles in the New York theater and on television. Lenny eats heartily and with pleasure. He wears a bright pink shirt open at the neck. He continually interjects comments and continually exudes vitality. Little Nina jumps up and walks to the piano. She strikes a few notes, then returns to her seat. "Mummy, I haven't touched the piano in years either!" she announces.

After dinner Lenny goes to the piano and accompanies Felicia, Jamie, my wife, and me in a reading of Pergolesi's *Stabat Mater*, which Jamie has brought along from New York. The singing is middling, but Lenny at the piano is fierce and intense. He cues his singers, screams at errors, prods more volume out of everyone, sings the impossible passages himself. He stops for no one. He goes right through the score with a running commentary on the beauty of this or that passage. It's a fairly long work, but Lenny sees it through to the end. There's no stopping—ever. Finally it's over.

Complete exhaustion on the part of singers. Lenny is ready to try it again. "Are you mad?" says Felicia. Everyone scurries to a couch or chair. Lenny gets up from the piano and joins us. Coffee is served to the adults. Soon Felicia sends the children off to bed. A few complaints from Jamie; she wants to stay up. She gets five minutes more. Then off she goes. Felicia and my wife now say good night. Lenny and I remain sitting in the living room.

It is very quiet now and he becomes somewhat somber. The mood has changed. I look at Leonard Bernstein. He sits here, three thousand miles away from New York, away from a life charged with incredible activity, a life that has included ten years as the conductor of the New York Philharmonic—the longest period anyone has held this post. Earlier in the year he had announced that he would retire as director of the Philharmonic at the end of the 1969 season. It would not be a total retirement (he will be Conductor Laureate for life), but he would no longer head the orchestra he has made one of the world's greatest. "Why are you quitting the Philharmonic?" I asked him. "Are you glad about it?"

"I'm glad I took the orchestra. And I'm glad I'm leaving the orchestra," he said. "As for the years I spent with it, I don't regret them at all.

"Of course, there are times when I think of what I could have written in that decade, especially if I had kept going from the moment of *West Side Story*, which was a kind of crucial moment in American musical theater, I think. It's very easy to speculate and to say, 'Ah, by now what would have happened!' Maybe nothing would have happened. But I thought at the time that the way was open for a gradual and sure development of an American theater form, which would become increasingly serious and complicated, but always in vernacular terms.

"But I had gotten to a point where I felt

at loose ends, even though what I was doing was very successful. I was trying to combine composing and conducting and playing the piano and television and all the rest of it in a way which had become confusing for me, because I had no center to my life. I was all over the place; I was feeling tired. And at that moment the New York Philharmonic came with this offer to succeed Dimitri Mitropoulos—to share a year with him first and then succeed him.

"After much thought I did accept it. I had talked with Felicia endlessly about it. She finally advised me to take it because it did seem to supply the locus that had been missing. I wanted some kind of central, settled feeling around which I could do the peripheral things. But it meant accepting the inevitable truth that now composing would be a peripheral thing. I've often asked myself whether that indicated something about me as a composer. If I were really an honest-to-God composer would I have accepted that job at that time?

"In spite of these musings and faint regrets, I have loved the Philharmonic. The past ten years have been immensely rewarding."

Bernstein paused, the musings and faint regrets reflected on his face. When Bernstein took over the Philharmonic in 1957 it was anything but an orchestra of refinement and polish.

This was in part due to Mitropoulos' relationship with the orchestra. A man committed to conducting and very little else, he had great musical intellectuality as well as a photographic brain. He devoted his life to studying scores, and it became obvious that only the most challenging works interested him. Mitropoulos became increasingly interested in twelve-tone music because of the challenge and because few other conductors were playing it at the time. In this way he alienated his audi-ences. Attendance at the Philharmonic dropped miserably. What is more, the sound of the orchestra deteriorated, primarily because Mitropoulos was not a disciplinarian. He did not insist on things. He was satisfied to secure from his men brilliant dynamic effects, for which he had a genius. But rhythmically and in ensemble the orchestra usually sounded poorly.

Recalling those years, Lenny observed, "As time went on, Dimitri began to hear more and more in his head what it was he conducted, rather than what was actually coming out. This, combined with his sweet, relaxed relationship with the orchestra, led to something awful, which was the men taking advantage of him, their not ever practicing, their not even trying to be in tune, their not trying to be together. It was a kind of laissez-faire. That is what I came to, with empty houses as a result.

"I did not set out to transform the Philharmonic. What I did try to do was to bring more discipline into the proceedings, to try to make the men play in tune, to try to make them listen to each other, and have some sort of ensemble feeling. To try to make them not be a bunch of boisterous kids, which they had become with Dimitri.

"It was not easy for me to do, because I was much younger than many of the people in the orchestra, and, of course, younger than Dimitri. I was just thirty-nine. But it worked somehow. We had a honeymoon. Then there were times, after two or three years of euphoria, when discipline problems again arose, even as they had for Mitropoulos, because we were all so friendly.

"I had an extra problem, which was that most of the men in the orchestra had known me since I was twenty-five, when I was assistant conductor. So I was 'Lenny' to begin with.

"I don't know of any other conductor who has been called by his first name—and a diminutive thereof, to boot. Of course, some still call me Mr. Bernstein and others call me Maestro, but most call me Lenny and it has absolutely no tone of denigration. People don't understand this, because it sounds disrespectful, as though the musicians are not taking me seriously. But if that were true, how could we have lasted for more than one season?

"Anyway, there was no audience-orchestra relationship when I arrived. The audience felt remote and left out. People came to a concert and there would be Dimitri playing the Schnabel symphony, then a desultory performance of a Mozart, and the audience sort of sat there and heard desultory programs, although every once in a while brilliant performances—like his Mahler Ninth or his Mahler Fifth, *Wozzeck*, the *Lyric Suite,* things that really engaged him, and nobody could master them that way, and have such fluidity and such instinctive ease. It was really extraordinary. At those moments the orchestra would recover its old fire and love, and it would all work. Then he would go all overboard, program a piece by Ralph Shapey and cancel it the day before the performance because he had bitten off more than anybody could chew.

"As a result of this, with the exception of those very memorable moments, the concerts had become something of a bore. The audiences had drifted away and those that remained felt alienated."

Bernstein felt that somehow or other he had to bring the audience back to music. Thus, he initiated the practice of talking to the audience and, eventually, of changing the Thursday night concert into a kind of *Generalprobe,* or open dress rehearsal, in the European style, to which the critics might or might not come. This, he believed, would serve many purposes. And it did.

For one thing, it gave the orchestra an extra rehearsal. It gave it a run-through in public, which nearly all European opera companies and concert orchestras do, and it provided an evening which could be handled flexibly. Bernstein could speak, if he wished. He could give examples from the piano. After a while, the Thursday evening concerts, which had been sparsely attended, suddenly became the chicest thing in town. As time went on, the subscription audience, heretofore a rejected, bored assemblage, turned into a sophisticated and knowledgeable group of people. Soon the conductor no longer needed to speak to the audience.

"No," said Lenny, "I didn't have to do that anymore, because they had become quite hip, and they have remained hip ever since.

"I am going to go on conducting the New York Philharmonic every year—that's part of having been made Conductor Laureate. Otherwise our parting would have been too heartbreaking. Nobody could have stood it, including me. After all, one develops a tremendous family feeling and relationship over ten years. But my work is done there, really, as music director. I think that in the ten years I've accomplished all that I wanted to do.

"The orchestra is in marvelous shape. Morale is high. They play like angels, despite the attacks of critics, who are still in the habit of saying the Philharmonic doesn't play as well as Orchestra X. Don't forget that the orchestra has also become enormously sophisticated by listening to all these programs during which I addressed the audience, and also through the more than forty Young Peoples Concerts we did on television. And my continually teaching them at rehearsals—that has helped, too.

"I think that teaching is perhaps the essence of my function as a conductor. I share whatever I know and whatever I feel about the music. I try to make the orchestra feel it, know it, and understand it, too, so that we can do it together. That's really what it is. It's a kind of chamber-music operation in which we are all playing together. I never think that they are there and I am here. Never. The whole joy of conducting for me is that we breathe together. It's like a love experience."

Bernstein grows wistful and silent. To leave the orchestra will be a wrench. And the men will surely feel the loss, as well. The vast expansion of the Philharmonic's activities under Bernstein has greatly increased their income. Moreover, they have come to regard him not only as a conductor, but also as a friend, confessor, psychiatrist. And administrative problems have taken more time, energy, and soul searching than even Lenny had anticipated.

"It's another reason I've had to resign," he told me. "The personnel part of it. The changes. When somebody retires, for example, and there's an opening. Does the next man in line go into that place, or do you hold auditions? If you get a new person, do you put him at the end and let him advance by seniority? What if the person next in line isn't, in your mind, worthy of that spot? What do you do? How do you explain it to him? This takes hours and days, and letters and phone calls, and personal meetings and tears. I mean, you can't ask X to audition at this point. He's

been at the Philharmonic twenty years. It's very ticklish, the whole personnel thing.

"But there is another important reason I've decided to resign: I lack somebody to champion. When I think back on the years of Koussevitzky, who proudly brought forth one Copland symphony after another, Roy Harris, Bill Schuman, Prokofiev, Stravinsky! He had all these glorious pieces. That period is over. When I came to the Philharmonic, I was expecting something like that to happen, and I find it so terribly disappointing that it hasn't —not really. I don't have anybody to champion. Nor do I have any cause to champion—a movement, a group of composers, a school."

It was getting very late. Lenny had, of course, warned me, even before we got to Italy, that many of our talks would more than likely take us late, late into the night. Lenny can't sleep. He is an insomniac of long standing. I, on the other hand, have no such problem and there were nights when I could barely keep my eyes open. But this was quickly remedied when I took recourse to certain little pills that gave the words wakefulness and alertness whole new meanings.

There were many more things I wanted to know about Bernstein's years with the Philharmonic, but Lenny did look very tired and another day was almost upon us.

3. Beside the pool. Lenny has decided to go diving. Earlier that morning he raced his Maserati to the local diving-goods store in nearby Orbetello. He returns with all kinds of gear and equipment. He has outfitted himself completely: from fifty-pound air tanks to waterproof watch, from rubber suit to depth gauge. Felicia and the children keep reminding Lenny of his bad back—indeed, about the fact that he knows very little about ocean diving.

Lenny's brother Burton—everyone calls him Burtie or B.B.—has come by to watch Lenny take wild chances. He jokes about it, scaring Lenny about the possible consequences. But Lenny turns a deaf ear to all admonitions. He can't wait to dive into the sea. After some preliminary sessions in the pool and a cursory glance at a diving manual, he plunges into the Tyrrhenian and is gone for a long, suspenseful time.

Lenny is a stubborn man. He must succeed. He does not relish defeat. In a way, he is fearless. But he is stubborn. When he rose to the surface after each diving bout, his back went out even more, and there followed hours of gloom, pain, and depression.

Yet again and again the sea drew him close. A few days after the first dives, Bernstein purchased a boat, the one that came with the villa having sprung a mysterious leak. He bought a Zodiac, one of those gray little inflatable rubber boats. And for it he bought an expensive new motor—which wouldn't start. I saw him sitting in the boat, pulling in vain at the starter cord. With each frantic pull, with each wrenching of the body, with each curse, Lenny became more enraged. He stormed from the boat, walked into the villa, refused lunch, and shut himself in his studio for the better part of the day. To a man to whom response means so very much, this was the kind of rejection that could throw him into despair.

Hoping to break his dark mood, I ventured into the studio. It was empty. But looking out of the window, I saw Lenny sitting in a swing-chair set up in an arbor. He was deeply engrossed in a book. I went up to him. He looked up in the friendliest manner. Obviously his rage with the nonfunctioning motor had passed. For the moment he was on to something far more engaging. He was reading *The Memoirs of Hadrian*, the novel by Marguerite Yourcenar, and he wanted to talk about it.

"This is a gloriously written book," he said. "I could read you whole chapters—and, amazingly, each line has some application to the way I've been feeling lately.

"Early in the book, Hadrian is talking about the three ways he has of knowing anything. One is self-observation, another is the observation of others, and the third is reading. But he finds books quite unsatisfactory because they always take a point of view. He ends that section by saying, 'I take little confidence in a world without books. But reality is not to be found in them, because it is not their whole. Direct observation of man is a method still less satisfactory, limited as it is to the cheap reflections which human malice enjoys.'

"Now here comes a part I'd like to quote you: 'As to self-observation, I make a rule of that, if only to come to terms with that individual with whom I must live up to my last day. But an intimacy of nearly sixty years' standing leaves still many chances for error. When I seek deep within me for knowledge of myself, what I find is obscure, internal, unformulated and as secret as any complicity.'

"That's exactly what I wanted to tell you the other night when you said, 'dig deep into yourself and tell me'—and this is what I find: obscure, unformulated, and secret. It's very hard to find out what goes on inside. I have a feeling that, with the exception of maybe Gide, or one or two people who really wrote a journal every single day, religiously, and made a habit of it, and said everything over a period of many years, that most men, or women, even at the age of sixty, are kind of faking it. They are being merely literary when they claim to discover real clues and essences in their own lives. I mean, to be truly honest you have to find it obscure, or internal, and so on, because one is not that consistent—one is not that much the same from day to day, or hour to hour, or month to month, for that matter. And therefore it's only a regular journal of some sort—or daily confession, or description, or interview, or whatever—that can begin to give you any kind of broad picture."

Lenny continued reading aloud from *The Memoirs of Hadrian*. His resonant, always expressive voice seemed to be in the act of discovering for him an ancient alter ego. He kept identifying with Hadrian's thoughts, ideas, and feelings, and commented on passages that he saw as relevant to his own state of mind. Finally, he laid the book aside and lit a cigarette, puffing on it slowly and thoughtfully. I sensed that Leonard Bernstein's mood was now imperceptibly changing. The day had not begun well for him. He had looked forward to spending hours on his boat and now a sudden, deep depression assailed him.

"That last line of Hadrian's I read you: 'It seems to me as I write this hardly important to have been emperor.' It really grabs me. I mean, these times, which are so dreamlike—one can't fathom them or take them seriously America is in the throes of a civil war this morning, and here we are, thousands of miles away reading about it, and shaking our heads, and saying, 'Anyone for water-skiing?' in the next breath. It's unreal.

"And so, as we sit here, for example, it seems hardly important to me that I'm the conductor of the New York Philharmonic, or that I'm a composer of any note at all, or that my existence on earth matters enough to talk about. This is one of the things that I warned you about at the very beginning: that it's very hard for me to feel the importance of all this.

"The world is on the verge of collapse. It's always, I suppose, been on the verge of collapse. But especially now, it's worse than ever, because of the multiplying nuclear arsenals and the total unpredictability of statesmen who are hardly statesmen-like. Perhaps, even worse, because of their very *pre*dictability. The farcical, cynical way everything is being handled. The massive lie that is constantly being told. How can one feel that one is a part of anything real? I can't.

"I'm constantly getting letters telling me how important it is that I do what I do. I can't even answer these. I feel they are so peripheral and far away from what's really going on. And what's really going on is a kind of living from day to day, right now. I feel of no importance at all. So it's very hard to talk about myself as though I mattered.

"I really can't reflect back. All I can do is reflect on the moments, as they go by, and try to extrapolate, as they say in *Partisan Review*, from these moments what the rest of my life must really be like, when I'm too busy to observe it.

"For example, I find it very difficult to rest—and I'm in a period of rest. I find it hard to sleep at night or nap during the day. Much more important to me are things like the boat, errands—like the car trunk that has to be fixed.

"I've been here two-and-a-half weeks now. So far it has not turned out at all the way I foresaw it in the middle of hectic activity: a kind of Eden-like calm and bliss, in which one will lie in the sun, or sit in the shade, or float in the water—and all these thoughts will come to you, all these ideas, musical inspirations, and what-not, that will be bubbling up. Instead, everything gets more and more gray and opaque and vague. I imagine if I stayed on another three or four months, it would get that much vaguer, that much more opaque."

Bernstein gets up. We walk into his studio. It's a smallish room, dominated by a Bechstein grand piano. There is a desk and an easy chair. Scattered on the desk are dozens of unanswered letters, music manuscript paper, books, newspapers, memorandums. Lenny goes to his desk and notes that he has not sealed a letter he had written some hours earlier. He picks it up. It is a letter to the wife of Egon Hilbert, director of the Vienna Opera. (Hilbert, ailing at the time the letter was written, was to die of a heart attack the following winter.)

"This letter also sort of sums up the way

I've been feeling these days,'' says Lenny.

Dear Gretl,

You must not be impatient about my letter-writing, nor draw mistaken conclusions from my silence. It is a silence of temporary withdrawal from the world into a sleeping life of sun, water, boats, family. No music, no thoughts, no planning, and hardly any communication with the world I've left. I don't know if you can understand how extremely important this period is for me, and how hard it is for me to write a letter. I've hardly written to my own parents. I haven't looked at a page of music—although the three volumes of Der Rosenkavalier *sit reprovingly on my piano. I have written not a note of my own music. My reading is reduced to letters, newspapers, and a slow rereading of* Hadrian's Memoirs. *It is all like a machine that has slowed down to a bare minimum. My constant companion is my son Alexander with whom I live in and on the water, and to whom I give occasional Hebrew lessons. This is all very necessary—this great* rallentando, *and it does not mean that I am happy in my resting. I have never really been happy except working. But it is a kind of slow, depressed happiness. As you see, it is very hard to describe. But I am trying to describe it to you, in order to explain why I cannot at this moment think clearly about* Meistersinger *or concert programs, or make relevant decisions. I'm sure that this period of Pause will soon be over and I will tell you everything. Meanwhile, I love to hear from you, I rejoice in the news of Egon's progress and send him my love. Poor Helmut, and poor Gretl, in that* Hitze! *I pray that Egon is soon well enough so that you can both leave Vienna for the cool hills and have your own* Pause, *your own* rallentando. *It is so necessary in this mad, sinister world.*

4.

Mornings at the Bernstein villa in Ansedonia always began with the phone ringing. The staff —maid, cook, gardener, laundress, plus Julia, the children's nurse brought from New York —were trained to answer the phone with care to ward off summer intruders and to take detailed messages. Lenny and Felicia seldom answered the phone themselves. Invitations to cocktail parties were turned down. The Bernsteins don't enjoy them. Only a few dinner invitations were accepted or made. These were usually with Burtie and his family, with Donald and Luisa Stewart (who shared their house with the Burton Bernsteins), or with my family and me.

But some of the phone calls were from friends or acquaintances from whom the Bernsteins were delighted to hear and who were promptly invited to the villa. Adolph Green and Betty Comden, whom Lenny has known for over thirty years and with whom he wrote *On the Town* and *Wonderful Town* were, of course, welcomed with open arms by all the Bernsteins. Indeed, Adolph Green had been to Israel with Lenny prior to his arrival in Ansedonia and remained with the Bernsteins for a number of days. Betty Comden and her husband, Steven Kyle, were vacationing in the area. They too stopped by for a few days. On one memorable occasion, Charles Chaplin, his wife Oona, and two of their teen-age daughters —Josephine and Victoria—came to dinner. (The evening proved memorable because it turned out to be a Chaplin-Bernstein festival of high-powered storytelling, music-making, and mad cutting up.)

The Bernsteins invited Priscilla and Eric Smith (he's connected with English Decca) to spend a few days with them. Martha Gellhorn, an old friend of Lenny's and Felicia's, came to visit, as did the Princess Lily Schoenburg, whom the Bernsteins know from Vienna. Mrs. Gaea Pallavicini, from Rome, paid several visits. Thomas Schippers and his wife stopped one afternoon for tea. And one of the Bernsteins' neighbors in Ansedonia, Mrs. Alice Thorne, a wealthy American who lives in Italy, was a frequent visitor. But even so there were long stretches when the Bernsteins saw no one.

Because of his insomnia, Lenny rose at noon. The very first thing he would do was to plunge into the sea for a swim. Later he would eat breakfast consisting of two raw eggs (he drinks them out of the shell), fresh fruit, and coffee. During breakfast he read his mail—stacks of it forwarded to him from New York, or sent to him from all corners of the world.

There were invitations to guest-conduct with major orchestras, invitations to write the scores of any number of films, musicals, or operas, invitations to write major compositions for major occasions. Lenny usually read his mail with a sort of summer languor. He could not bring himself to answer most of it. He wished to be left in peace, at least during his vacation. Stacks of letters remained unattended on his desk, all to be answered eventually, but not now.

Felicia, an early riser, would by this time be swimming in the pool, or be off with Jamie for some shopping in Orbetello or Porto Ercole, or, as was often the case, be sitting before her small easel, painting a portrait of Nina, Alexander, or Jamie.

Luncheons, on the other hand, were always full of talk, and, usually, full of excitement. In fact, lunchtime at the Bernsteins often became a hilarious battle of wits. Lenny involved himself with everything—the food, the appearance and behavior of his children, the weather, the mood Felicia was in. There was no question but that he encouraged response, and

he usually got it in lively, sometimes devastating doses. Few meals were consumed without at least one word-game in process. Lenny has a passion for them and Jamie is particularly brilliant at games like mental Jotto. There were times when these games became so compulsive that Felicia insisted they be stopped. But Lenny wouldn't hear of it. He went on with a zest and enthusiasm that bordered on the irritating.

Then, again, there were the simple questions answered in marathon detail. Jamie might ask the meaning of a Latin word, say, *genus*. Lenny was not satisfied merely to give the simple meaning of the word. He would begin by tracing its origins, explain all its forms, and find myriad examples of its usage in English, as well as in other languages. He was, in short, exasperatingly thorough—and always precise.

I recall Alexander asking Lenny one day just who Salome was. With characteristic enthusiasm, Lenny embarked on her story. He began with the Bible and ended with her appearance as the heroine of Richard Strauss' famous opera. Salome's various avatars were gone into in the greatest psychological detail, not excluding literary and art-historical allusions to her. The explanation lasted a good hour and culminated in Lenny's going to the piano and playing and singing several passages from the opera. It was an exhilarating experience, and Alexander—wide-eyed and smiling—was suddenly the world's best-informed little boy on the story of Salome.

Luncheon over, the Bernsteins usually scattered into their various afternoon activities. Lenny and Alexander would go off for their Hebrew lesson. Jamie retired to write letters or read. Nina would take her usual afternoon nap. And Felicia, sometimes accompanied by my wife Jane, would make a short excursion or two to ancient ruins in nearby villages. But one day we all went sailing. And on that day, Lenny seemed as content as I had ever seen him. He stretched out on the deck, closed his eyes, and let the sun and the water, and the wondrous silence of the boat's movement give him hours of pure pleasure. The day was still. Only a silken breeze stirred the sails. Lenny suddenly broke the silence. Addressing no one in particular he said, "Did you hear how the Russians announced that they had accelerated the speed of light? I heard it from a newspaper man I was with the other night. It was just a small bulletin, he said, but he had checked into it and it was true. It's amazing that the Russians themselves haven't made much more of it. It seems they sent a laser beam—that is, a light beam through a laser—and it arrived at its destination nine times sooner than a normal ray of light!

"This is an incredible thing, because the only constant we have in the world is the speed of light—C—which is an element of the famous formula E equals MC squared. If we don't have that constant anymore, it can be something else, and it's 'back to the old drawing board!' And yet, the atom has been split, and fission has been accomplished, and the bombs do go off, alas, based on that formula and its corollaries.

"But it's very exciting, because something must happen about time if the speed of light can be altered. It can be slowed. It can be accelerated. I don't know anything about it, I'm just trying to feel my way, but you begin to feel yourself being on the brink of an H. G. Wells novel...."

Lenny immersed in the phenomenon of time! This appeals to him. Lenny likes to think in cosmic terms. The idea of the far-reaching thought or gesture appeals to him. He enjoys ferreting out the grand design in the grain of sand. He falls silent again. The boat slowly passes a breathtaking series of jagged caves jutting out of the sea. In the distance behind them, Monte Argentario forms a panoramic shell of deepest greens and browns. The sky is cloudless and almost white with the fierce sun. Felicia exclaims and marvels over the view before us. Her response to nature is very strong. Far stronger than Lenny's. She is the visual member of the family. Lenny seems hardly aware of the land- and seascapes that present themselves at every turn of our heads. It prompts me to question him about it.

"I don't respond primarily to the panoramic in nature," he answers. "That sort of thing doesn't overwhelm me. Rather, I look at nature microscopically. I looked at a cactus needle for a half hour the other day. That's what fascinates! You know the old thing of a blade of grass—Whitman's blade of grass. I can never get over those things. And I look at the way sea urchins are made. And not only do I study them, but I love eating their contents. I am fascinated by them and by every creature and every piece of vegetable matter in the world. I can never get over it, because I always feel that somewhere in these living things you might find a key to yourself.

"I always feel I'm on the verge of seeing something—in a sea urchin, in a blade of grass, in a cactus needle, in a trumpet vine, or flower. Why is it made this way? How does it know how to do that? Why does it bud this way, or smell this way? How does it know exactly when to fall off and die?

"When I submerge myself in nature—in the water, for example—I feel I'm on the brink of knowing something, of discovering something, some secret which will tell me my identity with all this. That would bring me peace. But I'm never let in on the secret; I am only teased by feeling close to it.

"Actually, my greatest joys with nature are those in which I feel myself being a part of it.

Such as right now, on this sailboat. Moments like these are like skiing moments, or diving moments when you become part of nature.

"It's half a passive feeling—of being 'taken' by the hill, by the current, by the wind. But the other half is you. You're doing it you're also active. It's a marvelous feeling. It's part of the state of being in balance, a beautiful feeling of *bien-être,* of being exactly equal parts of active and passive, of being conditioned by the natural forces around you, and of conditioning them somehow.

"No, the panoramic aspects of nature—the vastness of the heavens, the wheeling firmament and all that, that doesn't excite me half so much as the feeling of participating in nature.

"But the other night, when I couldn't sleep, I sat out on the terrace and looked up at the sky, and concentrated on one star, and tried to imagine what it is, when it is, if it's there, really. And I watched it fade as the dawn came up. That's an extraordinary experience: when you can't see it anymore and yet you see it blinking. You don't know if you are seeing it blink, or if it's an after-image in your brain. That's a very magical moment: when you're not sure whether it's dark or light, and when you're watching one star, in its terms watching the whole firmament. But I find this very hard to articulate...."

Yet he articulated it all very well. Lenny is never at a loss for words. And he chooses them with care because he has an almost obsessive need to communicate his knowledge and his feelings with utmost precision.

We sail homeward. A slight chill fills the air. Soon the sun will set and the colors of the sky, the sea, and the coastline will intensify and deepen. And this long and quiet afternoon sailing on the Silver Coast with the Leonard Bernsteins calmly comes to an end.

5. As the summer progressed, I would casually mention to Lenny that we had never really finished our talk about his years with the Philharmonic. I wanted to know much more: how he prepared for a concert; what his feelings were about conducting; what happens to him when he conducts.

Lenny hears these questions, but he does not respond immediately. You talk about something else. You take a dip in the pool. You have some tea with the family, and perhaps later play a four-hand Mozart sonata, with Lenny at your side teaching you the finer points of four-hand piano playing.

The pace is always leisurely though no less intense, because with Lenny around an indescribable something always keeps you on your toes. Even in his quietest moments, Lenny exudes a certain electricity.

One day I found Lenny sitting on the terrace, looking searchingly into the distance. I sat down beside him. We hadn't talked seriously for days. He did not acknowledge my presence, but, of course, knew I was sitting there beside him. Suddenly, still looking into the distance, he intoned:

"I'm talking to you from way out there.... I've been gone a long time and I may never get back.... It's cold out there.... It's endlessly dark and endlessly light.... On the side away from the sun the temperature is minus 2000 Fahrenheit! On the side toward the sun.... Ahhh! It's weightless out there.... You want to talk about what? Rituals?"

We both burst out laughing. "You remembered!" I said. Some days before, I had asked him how he prepares for a concert, if he went through a routine, or a ritual.

"I don't think I have as much of a ritual as other conductors," Lenny began. "The one thing that has a ritual quality about it is showering and dressing before a concert, which is not a ritual in the sense that there is an absolute pattern that has to be followed. As a matter of fact, as likely as not, the children will be in the bathroom chatting with me. But there is something ritualistic in the act of preparation itself, which is almost priestlike—before I approach the altar. I don't know where this comes from. But there is something about getting scrupulously clean, squeaky clean. It's a cleansing ritual. It's a becoming-worthy-of-entering this holy of holies, that everything you put on must be absolutely spotless, like priestly garments.

"Most conductors I've observed dress in the tailcoat they wore at the last concert. They just hang it up after a concert at the hall and put it on again to go on stage. I could no more do that than I could walk out in a bathing suit. Everything must be new—clean from skin outward. It is a sign of the general feeling I have before a concert. And that's my only ritual—oh, except this:

"When Koussevitzky died I was given a pair of his cuff links. I wear them always when I conduct. This has developed into something like a superstition—the only one I have. Anyway, I must conduct every concert with those cuff links. They are very precious to me—simple, square, gold cuff links. But they were his, and I always kiss them before going out on the stage.

"Rodzinski, I believe, never conducted without a revolver in his back pocket. I don't know what that meant. Also, one was asked to kick him backstage before he entered. I was asked several times to do this. A good luck kick. I don't know where that comes from, either. But he had millions of such superstitions. Every-body has got something. But the extent of mine is this little pair of cuff links and absolute cleanliness.

"The irony is that by the time I get to the hall my clothes are usually quite wrinkled from the ride in the car. If I had any sense, I would dress at the hall. But I like to leave the house ready for the concert. I don't like hanging around in the dressing room. Many conductors arrive very early. Toscanini always used to appear hours in advance. He'd dress there—bring everything—because he wanted to be in the hall, to know that he was safely there and sit and think and whatever.

"I don't arrive in my dressing room and have an absolutely quiet period of meditation, or anything like that. On the contrary, there are usually all kinds of people waiting for me, either to greet me, or with problems that must be solved, decisions that must be made."

Before he faces the orchestra, Leonard Bernstein is strangely calm and reserved. It is an inner calm, nurtured by purpose and expectation. Just before he goes on, he likes to have a last-minute look at the score. He does not study it, but he looks at it, getting very close to it again. In fact, the last thing that happens is that the librarian comes for the score—if Bernstein is using one—and puts it on the podium. Usually, Lenny will say to him, "Wait a minute. Just another second. Yes, I'll give it to you in a moment." It's like a last good-bye before he sees it again out there in the bull ring. And as he put it, "It's really more like touching it with your eyes."

Bernstein studies his scores at home. And the way he studies them is a small lesson in compulsion. What he does first is what he does first when he begins a novel: He sneaks a look at the end. He's dying to see how it comes out. Lenny loves last lines and last bars, last statements. From there, he usually riffles backwards. Oddly enough, he seems to get more of an impression of the general form that way than when he reads forward. Having gone through it once, he then goes back to the beginning and really studies.

To mark scores, he uses a colored pencil—red on one end, blue on the other. Anything in red is meant for the librarian to copy into the musicians' parts. These are usually special accents, bowings, and other modifications of dynamics. The blue pencil is for his own markings. He uses it to indicate phrasing, to outline the harmonic rhythms—in general to set off the long musical sentences and paragraphs. Bernstein thickens the bar lines at the dividing points, making a kind of map of the score. He also uses this blue pencil to call attention to not immediately obvious dynamic subtleties, to instrumentation that might not be seen offhand, to something he might want to call to the men's attention. These markings are used mostly in rehearsal; by the time of the performance, Bernstein is no longer dependent on them.

When he conducts with a score, it is finally taken from Bernstein and placed on the podium. Then, as in the theater, someone calls, "Five minutes, maestro." The five minutes up, that same someone says, "Time, maestro." At this point, the Philharmonic's assistant manager takes Bernstein down the elevator and delivers him to the personnel manager, who is waiting in the wings, and who then gives the concertmaster the direction to go on the stage and tune up the orchestra. When the orchestra is tuned, the personnel manager quiets the orchestra by shushing it violently from the wings. He then gives a signal to the light-board man to put the house down. He bows Lenny on. And Bernstein is delivered into the jaws of the lion.

(In Europe, the conductor is clapped on—the applause is started backstage. This is the signal for the audience to begin clapping, and the conductor goes on.)

And so, Bernstein walks to the podium and bows. At a Friday afternoon subscription concert, with an audience of three thousand ladies who applaud through their gloves, so that one hears more jingling of bracelets than clapping of hands, Lenny may bow only briefly and turn to his appointed task. But then, for the duration of the concert, Leonard Bernstein is immersed.

"From then on I can't tell you what happens," he says. "One could make metaphors about it. I mean, you are swimming in the womb, you are in the labyrinth being led by Ariadne's cord, you are deeply in something. This cord of Ariadne, of course, is a multiple cord, all the various strands of the work that you are doing are leading you, and all of you is being led. There isn't any other place. There isn't any other time or geography except this inner geography, this journey.

"The orchestra never disappears. I mean, one is not alone with Brahms or whomever. We are all alone with him. There is a tremendous involvement with the men. Actually, there is no such thing as remaining alone in ecstatic glory. The audience may disappear from consciousness. But the men remain with me.

"When it's over, and you've really been away in the labyrinth, it's really an effort to come back. I once had one of my little verbal game fantasies about coming back to the here and now. I thought 'here-now' transposed is 'now-here,' and 'now-here' put together is 'nowhere,' and I found some kind of profound meaning in that, because compared to where you've been, 'now-here' is, indeed, 'nowhere.'"

I asked Lenny if his performances are ever affected by his own moods. "Not in the easy sense that when you're feeling depressed, it will show. Or that that's a good time to conduct Tchaikovsky's Sixth, because it's depressed music. It's not that easy, and it's not that one-to-one. As a matter of fact, when you're in a very strong mood, a very positive mood, it may be exactly the right time to conduct Beethoven's Funeral March.

"I know that in general the stronger you feel, and the readier you feel, the more gism you have for the performance—the better it will be no matter what the music is."

After a concert, Bernstein loves to receive friends in the Green Room. He loves congregating with them, joking and talking about the concert. He offers drinks and retires to his dressing room, where his dresser helps him back into his street clothes. Bernstein then goes to the outer reaches of the Green Room where people are always waiting for him to sign autographs. Lenny usually spends a good deal of time with them. Besides giving autographs, which a lot of conductors don't do, he chats with them. He is interested in knowing what they think, how they've reacted to the concert, if they're excited, and why.

During this period his friends in the Green Room wait for him. They are usually restive because Lenny takes too long chatting with his fans. Finally he returns. He and his friends go out, to a restaurant, a film, a round of discotheques. Or he may take his friends back to his house. "I don't like to go to bed. That's out of the question, because I'm always full of adrenaline and everything is pumping away. There are times when I've just gone home alone—although there's something rather anticlimactic about that. Sometimes I go home and immediately study the next program."

6. Midnight. The lights of Porto Ercole flicker dimly across the stretch of sea seen from the terrace. Above those distant flickering lights, Monte Argentario looms like some awesome night creature risen from the sea. It is a windless, very silent moment. Although Lenny sits quite near me, I can barely make out his face, which is now very deeply tanned. His back has hurt him all day. It has wearied him. He sits smoking a cigarette, which, as he draws on it, momentarily illuminates his eyes. There is something profoundly sad about Lenny tonight. There are long sighs and long silences. We both sit, quietly sipping our drinks. The ice in our glasses makes a startlingly loud sound in this silence.

Leonard Bernstein is depressed and sad. "I've written only two works in the last ten years," he says. "Since I took over the Philharmonic, at the point when I finished *West Side Story*, I've done just those two, neither of them for the theater. *Kaddish* and *Chichester Psalms*. Both Biblical in a way. Something seems to keep making me go back to that book. And there was *Jeremiah*.

"Of course, it all ties back to Daddy. That whole tremendous influence. It's pure ambivalence. I think the two poles of the ambivalence are not just poles, but are interdependent and mutually influential, if you know what I mean. I'm sure that if you investigate it, it becomes a tangled neurotic knot.

"For example, I must feel a certain guilt about my father, about having resented him, feared him so when I was a child. Because he opposed my music, because he didn't seem to understand me.

"It doesn't mean I had a compensating, equivalent dependence, or an elaborate, exaggerated love for my mother. I was very fond of her. But it isn't that I threw myself completely on my mother's side and rejected my father, although she did have much greater sympathy for the music, for the whole artistic idea.

"And yet my father impressed me enormously. I admired him. I learned so much from him. His knowledge was enormous—extremely limited and circumscribed by Talmudic studies, yet within that limited area his knowledge was enormous. His intelligence was equally enormous. The breadth of his reasoning—which is a Talmudic quality—made him in every sense a man of God. He is a deeply religious man. Highly moral."

Bernstein paused. I wondered aloud whether this ambivalent feeling toward his father still showed itself in any way. "In some minor ways, yes," he answered. "To this day I have not been able to rid myself of certain little patterns whose origins I clearly see. For example, I never play golf. I don't want to hear about pinochle. Canasta, poker, bridge, anything you want, but I don't want to know about pinochle because that was his game. Really, to reach my age and still carry those ridiculous taboos around! It's stupid. I mean, man's power to change being his divine element—his divine faculty—why can't I have changed enough to have thrown off these prejudices against such innocent things as golf and pinochle?

"As time went on, he mellowed very much and I understood him much better. We became very good friends—which we are now. I came to love him and understand his terrible faults and foibles and weaknesses—and the pain and the suffering he went through in his life."

Lenny told me that from the very first his father had pinned his hopes on one of two things for him. Either to go into his business or become a rabbi. The idea of Lenny becoming a musician was both distasteful and depressing to him. It had to do with his own somewhat limited points of reference. In his day, to be a musician meant somebody sitting in the lobby of a hotel, playing in a trio. In eastern Europe a musician was a *klesmer,* a sort of wandering minstrel little better than a beggar, who would go from town to town looking for weddings and feasts, and be thrown a crust, or be invited to sit down and have something to eat for his labors. A *klesmer!* His son was going to be a *klesmer!* Never!

Lenny's mother, on the other hand, was never quite so adamant. She seemed, in fact, to encourage Lenny's earliest musical interests.

"My mother insists that I was always very musical, that even as a child, before I could speak, I was drumming out rhythms on the windowsill—that when I heard a piano I'd go mad. Or the radio. Those were the very early days of radio. I can remember radio at the age of eight, or so: a huge Atwater-Kent with a big horn and three dials, which took hours to tune in a station. I can remember being excited by music on that. I think my mother may be a Monday-morning quarterback, if you know what I mean: rationalizing backward from the present and deciding in *Hintersicht* that I was always terribly musical. Maybe she's right. I know that the family was not musical. We never had music in the house. We had no piano. We had a phonograph, but it played only 'Barney Google.'

"I never knew there was a world of music, a world of concerts, or opera. I never was taken to any. I had no notion that anything like this existed. I remember hearing, oh, Rossini overtures and such things on the radio and going mad with excitement. But still, nothing happened.

"And then one day, my Aunt Clara—my father's younger sister, and a remarkable woman—decided to move back to New York, where she had previously lived, and she didn't know what to do with some of her heavier articles of furniture. So she dropped some of them off in our house. A big lamp, a sofa—God knows what! But also a piano! An upright. An old-fashioned, heavy, carved, upright piano with a middle pedal which, when depressed, caused it to sound like a mandolin. Do you remember those mandolin pedals on the old pianos? Well, this thing was moved into our house and stationed in the hallway because there was no other place to put it. And I touched it. And that was that.

"From that day to this, it has been very hard to remove me from my keyboard. That's where I suddenly felt at the center of a universe I could control, or at least be at the center of, in the sense that I felt it revolving stably around me, instead of me being tossed around in it, which I had felt up to then.

"I was safe at the piano, for some reason. Even before I knew how to play it, I was improvising not only music but a system of music. I made my own system of harmony. Nobody ever taught me harmony till I was in college. I didn't know that you could study harmony. I found that there were chords that existed in a certain relation to one another—and I gave them names. I had 'finishing chords' and 'governing chords.' It's very funny that I came to the name 'governing' because dominant means governing. Subdominants became 'sort-of-governing chords,' some kind of variation like that. I found out later that my own terms matched almost exactly in spirit the official names for the chords. Then I had terms for modulating and keys; I don't know what they were anymore. But it was a rather complete system, as I discovered when I came to study harmony at Harvard.

"Between the ages of ten and twelve I was always fooling with the piano. At home nobody minded much, except that I used to do it too late and they would complain that it kept them up. It was a complaint that went on as long as I lived at home. 'Will you stop that infernal banging' department. 'Let somebody get some sleep around here!' It was very hard for me to stop."

Here Lenny paused. "I know it would have pleased my father deeply if I had become a rabbi," he said. "And there is a certain amount of rabbi in me which I get from him, of course. He is the son of a rabbi and he is very rabbinical in nature himself. If you say to him 'pass the salt,' he's already teaching you something: 'You know, Moses said about salt...' or whatever. I must say, I've inherited some of that. I do tend to be lecture-y and I love to teach. I also, I'm sure, bore people to death by giving lectures when all they want is a simple answer. I know this is true of my children. I do it constantly. It's part of my rabbinical streak.

"I suppose I could have made a passably good rabbi. However, there was no question of it, because music was the only thing that consumed me.

"I loved other things. I loved other studies. I was particularly taken with English literature and poetry. And languages. But music was a whole other thing. It wasn't a study, you see. It was a way of life.

"But as a child I had no musical taste. I had no way of having taste. I had no musical life except my own. I composed all the time. I wrote a piano concerto when I was thirteen. I found a page of it the other day. It looks like Liszt, Wagner, Grieg, Rachmaninoff. A caricature of those composers—but very passionate."

As Bernstein talked, recalling his very early past, his dark spirits lifted. There was something very young and very touching about him at this moment. Reliving these early years, he seemed filled with a youthful zest, with an enthusiasm that seemed quite different in quality than it is these days. Coming back to the subject of his father, he said, "My father made peace with me a long time ago. And these close to twenty-five years that I've been 'successful'—to use his terminology—he has lived on this.

"Of course, if anybody said to him now that he had ever stood in the way of my music, he wouldn't deny it, but he has ways of rationalizing. He had a marvelous line that was quoted in some interview: 'Well, how was I supposed to know that he was Leonard Bernstein!' He said that! It's very witty, actually."

Lenny laughed and I laughed, and, looking at our watches, we both saw how late it had gotten, and how the sky had turned very black, and how, in fact, it had gotten quite chilly. We went inside. Everyone, of course, was asleep. The only sound anywhere came from an electric ice-making machine near the bar in the living room. It periodically manufactured ice cubes which fell with insistent little thuds into a tray. It was a sound we came to know extremely well, as our middle-of-the-night talks progressed.

Despite the lateness of the hour, Lenny was not quite ready for sleep. The record album of *Kaddish* was lying on the sofa. Earlier on, I had listened to it again. Lenny picked up the album, then let it fall.

"I love *Kaddish*," he said, "but I'm not at all satisfied with the text. God knows I tried everything not to write it myself. You know, I worked with Robert Lowell and he actually wrote three poems for it, three beautiful poems, but they're lyric poems of a certain obscurity which would not have served the purpose of immediacy needed in the concert hall. They were too literary; he realized it, too. 'I'm not the man for you.' Finally, I had to do it myself. I worked very, very hard. Some of it is good. Some of it is much better than has been acknowledged by the angry critics. I've never seen criticisms so violent and personal as *Kaddish* had.

"Still, they are right about certain aspects of it, which are too immediate. In my fervor to make it immediately communicative to the audience, I made it overcommunicative, so that there are embarrassing moments. I know Felicia, who narrated it, had moments—overly verbose lines—that she simply couldn't speak. Eventually I did enormous cutting. But the text is still too overblown, still too corny. I do wish I could revise it, or find the perfect somebody who could revise it."

Suddenly Lenny said good night; he simply had to get to sleep, if he could.

7.

"I knew someone elegant was coming!" says Nina Bernstein, looking up from her five-year-old height into the faces of Charles Chaplin, Oona O'Neil Chaplin, and Josephine and Victoria Chaplin. The Chaplins, spending two weeks in Porto Ercole, have come to dine with the Bernsteins.

They arrive in their chauffeur-driven Rolls-Royce, an immense, black car—surely, for the duration of their stay, the biggest car on the entire Silver Coast. Its license plate bears the letters CC. And now here he stands, Chaplin, being greeted effusively by Felicia, Lenny, Jamie, Alexander, and Nina. Chaplin, the monument, in the warm embrace of Bernstein, the American Dream come true. The two had met very briefly once before, but, of course, each is acutely aware of the other's legend. Betty Comden Kyle and her husband Steve arrive to join the party. Everyone moves to the terrace for predinner drinks. Chaplin is in a light blue, short-sleeved sweater that buttons at the collar. He wears white trousers, and his sockless feet are comfortably protected in red leather house slippers. He is smiling, his blue, blue seventy-eight-year-old eyes still sparkling. The face is now worn, but the "little tramp" still lurks mischievously beneath it. He stands on this terrace, a little old white-haired gentleman with a protruding belly, and as we all look at him a deluge of memories spills to every corner of our minds like so many film clips projected at double speed by some fanatic Chaplin buff. He smiles at us all. Chaplin's smile begins coyly, then changes to reticence, then broadens into something bright, sunny, heartbreaking.

Oona Chaplin is wearing a short white belted cotton dress. She is matronly, but still lithe and fresh of face and body. Her jet-black hair is worn short now. It gives greater contour and decisiveness to her features. Her face reveals calmness and contentment. Eight children! A placid mother, but of late a somewhat apprehensive wife. Chaplin is growing old. Oona's eyes seldom leave his face. She serves as his memory as he recounts tale after tale. Certain details, certain names slip his mind. Oona Chaplin supplies them and the tales become more accurate, funnier.

Victoria and Josephine, sixteen and eighteen respectively, are teen-age goddesses. They offer delectable images of the miniskirted generation. Incredibly slim and long-legged, they seem utterly removed in time from their famous father. In fact, they admit to having joined their childhood school friends in the rope-skipping rhyme: "Charlie Chaplin went to France, to teach the girlies how to dance...." never quite aware that Charlie Chaplin was their very own father!

Dinner conversation centers on his films, his life, his thoughts, his feelings. Lenny is full of questions and he gives Chaplin the floor. The stories come fast and furious (Chaplin is a marvelous raconteur) and they are, for the most part, centered in the distant past. The present seems vaguer to Chaplin; it finds him somewhat irritated, dissatisfied. He tells of his dismay at the critical reception accorded *The Countess from Hong Kong*. "The film was brilliant," he says. "It was ten years ahead of its time!"

"Now, Charlie," says Oona, "that's a pretty extravagant statement for anybody to make." Chaplin says, "Perhaps, but the critics just didn't understand it. It was a charming love story taking place aboard ship—and a good comedy situation. What could be more charming than a lovely stowaway getting into the hair of an important statesman?"

Chaplin tells us he's planning a new film based on a mythological subject, to star his daughters Victoria and Josephine. "Not Geraldine?" someone asks. "Not for the moment," he answers. It seems Chaplin is not quite sold on Geraldine's acting talents, despite her current success on stage and screen. But Victoria and Josephine have no desire to become actresses. Victoria as yet has no idea what she wants to be, and Josephine is studying voice in the hope of making singing her career.

Dinner over, we move into the living room. Bernstein now suggests that Chaplin play some of his famous movie music. He leads him to the piano. Chaplin protests, but finally sits down and plays the themes from *Limelight* and *City Lights*. He plays them with a great deal of feeling and with a great many notes cascading across the keyboard. Lenny is elated. He sits down beside him. He then begins playing some of the music that usually accompanies the Chaplin one-reelers. Fast Spanish numbers, hurtling chase passages, and the like.

Chaplin gets up. He becomes even more elated than Lenny. Suddenly he's in the center of the living room going through some of the actions suggested by the music. He is transformed. He becomes the young Chaplin caught in a thousand dilemmas. He takes his little steps. He pivots. He reels. Lenny plays faster and faster. The company howls. The unpredictable has happened. Chaplin is performing and Lenny is goading him on. Oona laughs, but looks slightly concerned. Charlie is really exerting himself.

This over, Lenny embarks on a mock Italian opera. A superbly improvised Verdi opera, which becomes Donizetti, then Puccini. Chaplin becomes the compliant tenor. In mock-Italian he sobs out an aria. He moves from one side of the living room to the other. His actions mimic the crescendos and diminuendos of the music. His arms flail the air. He suddenly lifts a leg. In a moment, he is kneeling beside an empty chair. His voice becomes ever more tremulous. The aria becomes more and more impassioned. Quickly, he runs toward a window. The music becomes tragic. Chaplin clutches the curtains. He is about to climb them. Everyone screams with laughter. But the music now subsides. It is time for a long recitative. *"Uccidere! Uccidere!"* darkly intones Chaplin. His arm shoots threateningly toward the sky. But it falls heavily to his side, as despair overcomes him.

Lenny introduces a new aria. Chaplin is ready for it, singing with short little gasps of disillusionment. The aria grows in intensity. All at once, Betty Comden is at his side. She sings with him. The two clasp each other. In a very high soprano, Betty declares her love. They join in a mad, frenzied duet, which seems to end on the highest notes ever sung by living man, woman, or beast. Everyone, including Lenny at the piano, is completely overcome with laughter. Lenny rushes from the piano to embrace Chaplin.

It is an incredible performance, one that could not have taken place without the formidable drives that activate the two talented men.

The evening must end. Oona Chaplin rises and everyone knows it is time for Charlie Chaplin to get his rest. Still, the Bernsteins and the Chaplins chat a long while at the entrance of the villa, until the hundredth good night is said and the black Rolls-Royce moves out of the driveway and into the night.

"Someone Elegant" arrives: An Evening with Charlie Chaplin (and Daughter Josephine)

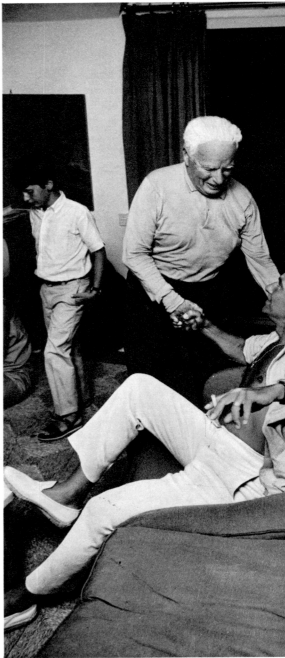

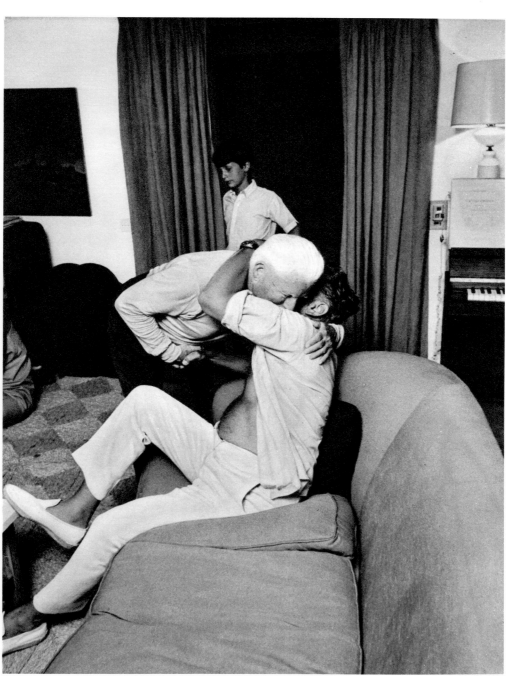

8.

"I've just mailed a letter to Aaron Copland. About half way through it I realized that it was all in telegraphic prose. It was full of 'can't sleep,' 'need rest,' et cetera. It's funny that I should have this desire to write to Aaron. I see him very rarely these days. I didn't write him anything of a particularly personal nature, nothing I couldn't say to somebody else. But I needed to say it to him. It's like a throwback to being nineteen or twenty."

Leonard Bernstein's friends are the friends he's always had. He is loyal and his feelings toward them seldom change. He may not see them regularly—everyone's life goes at its own pace or in its own direction—but Lenny's feelings for his friends are unchanging. Copland is such a friend—one of very long standing. The two have known each other for some thirty years.

Now, sitting on some rocks by the Tyrrhenian Sea, Lenny talks about the letter to Copland and drifts back into the past.

"He was a sort of very early father-confessor. Somebody I trusted enormously. No matter how insecure I felt, or how depressed, it was all right if I was hanging onto Aaron's arm, walking down the street. He was infallible. I'm sure that he influenced me much more than just in my music. I find myself still, so many years later, speaking phrases that are typically Aaron's.

"One thing that impressed me tremendously about Aaron was his plainness. It's true of his music and true of his speech, too. It's something distinguished. It's true of his life: very simple, homely, Lincolnesque, all those adjectives we've all used about him. That, I think, had a big influence on me, because I acquired almost a reverence for plainness of speech, for directness, which fitted in very well with my need for communicating with people. To speak as clearly as possible.

"But I suppose that at that point in my life I could have been influenced toward fanciness by people at Harvard, who were very fancy. Or toward a certain donnishness. Or a fad for using highly technical terms. Apparently I resisted that, because I don't think I ever do. I don't use 'in' words, or words that are bigger than I need; I don't think I do. That's all tied up with Aaron. As is the directness in the music, except that I went even further in using the vernacular. That is, it's not as transformed as it is in his music. Which is not a credit to me, by any means. It makes his music more art than mine is. It makes his music more durable, more interesting."

Copland gave Bernstein a way of looking at life, a concern with individual liberty and with the underdog, with minorities and with the fight for modern music. "At one point I suppose Aaron was a radical," continued Lenny, "but long before I knew him he had changed to a moderate, which he has remained to this day. Moderate to an extraordinary degree. I mean, he's Mr. Moderate. A well-balanced, considered man. Wise. Solomonic. Canny. He sees through a problem, sees through people's pretenses about problems and their fake solutions. I guess he is the most balanced man I've ever known. A private man. Special. A deeply lovable man. And so jocular. Such fun."

And so, Lenny wrote Copland a letter. Also because he had been wondering what Copland's new piece was like. The Philharmonic's 125th anniversary, to be celebrated in 1968, called for the commissioning of new works, among them a score by Aaron Copland. The piece eventually arrived in Ansedonia, and Lenny was delighted with it. He subsequently performed it with the Philharmonic (it was entitled *Inscape*), but its critical reception was somewhat less than overwhelming.

Before Bernstein had seen the work, he told

me that Copland had been having difficulty composing.

"When he has the premiere of a new piece, the young composers don't show up anymore—not the way they used to. When he did turn to twelve-tone music, it was already too late. The kids were already way ahead of him with something else. So I tend to think of him, in these later years, at some sort of impasse. I have asked him about it and he has said he doesn't have so much desire to compose anymore. His way is to say that most composers, with notable exceptions like Verdi, didn't live to compose much beyond the age of fifty-five or sixty. And here he is nearing seventy. He'll be sixty-seven this year. He said, 'You know, the urge isn't as strong as it used to be.'"

They met in 1937, on November 14, Copland's birthday. That date, November 14, was to mean a great many things in Leonard Bernstein's life, and it plays a role in Lenny's reluctant semibelief in the magic of numbers, in their almost occult involvement with fate and destiny. Exactly six years later, on November 14, 1943, Bruno Walter got sick and Leonard Bernstein had to take over the Philharmonic.

9.

The astonishing Philharmonic debut of Leonard Bernstein—aged twenty-five—on the afternoon of Sunday, November 14, 1943, is, of course, a matter of record. And yet even to think about it, here in sunny Ansedonia, throws Lenny into a certain ennui. He much prefers a long swim, or reading a book, or being with Felicia and the children, or working on the piano piece he's finally started. But I tell him that despite all the written reports of that extraordinary event, nothing could possibly compare with his own personal recollections of it. The details would be different, the nuances would alter, the very fact that he would be recalling it twenty-five years later would bring new insights into it. Besides, that debut proved to be one of the most thrilling stories in the annals of conducting. In fact, it changed the course of conducting in America. It is safe to say that were it not for Bernstein's prodigious success that afternoon, the possibilities for a young American conductor to make headway in a profession traditionally dominated by aging Europeans would continue to be negligible.

Lenny is reluctant. Besides, he feels that the years leading up to that memorable afternoon would need to be gone into—and in greatest detail. He would have to talk about his early acquaintance and apprenticeship with Dimitri Mitropoulos, Fritz Reiner, Serge Koussevitzky, and Artur Rodzinski.

Instead, he turns to me and asks: "Do you ever do British crossword puzzles?" We are sitting in his study, and there, lying on his desk, are copies of the *Observer*, the *Times*, and other London papers, each open to the puzzle page. Some of the crosswords have been started, others are finished, yet others are still untouched. "I find them excruciatingly difficult," I reply. "But why is it that you find puzzles so intriguing?"

Lenny answers: "Because they check out *right*, and on many levels of meaning. Whatever level you seek it on, it's right. It's the only thing in the world that is. Except music! The only thing in the world that comes out right. That checks and is impossible to fault. It's so satisfying, it makes you believe again in an ordered cosmos. These puzzles are a kind of anchor in a believable reality. I just adore doing them. I feel completely content."

Bernstein's almost compulsive delight in British crossword puzzles dates back to his years at the Curtis Institute in Philadelphia, where between 1939 and 1941 he studied conducting with Fritz Reiner and piano with Isabella Vengerova. As a Harvard graduate Lenny was disliked by the other Curtis students, most of them prodigies who had arrived in knee pants and who spent year after year learning their music and little else. They resented Lenny's superior airs, his incredible brilliance on all musical and nonmusical levels, and his teachers' response to this brilliance. The two years he spent at Curtis coincided with Randall Thompson's tenure as director of the Institute. Thompson, with whom Lenny studied orchestration, had also come from Harvard, was an academic kind of man, and a composer. Teacher and pupil inevitably became close friends and it was during this time that Thompson's enthusiasm for British crossword puzzles was transmitted to Bernstein.

The anti-Bernstein atmosphere at Curtis was strong enough to induce a mentally unbalanced student to buy a gun with which he planned to shoot not only Bernstein but also Reiner and Thompson. Luckily, the plan was discovered and the student shipped back home.

Bernstein had chosen Curtis at the suggestion and recommendation of Dimitri Mitropoulos, whom Lenny had met in Boston during his sophomore year at Harvard. This was a meeting that has marked Lenny for life, for it was Mitropoulos who first ignited his imagination in terms of conducting. Recalling the first concert he ever heard Mitropoulos conduct, Bernstein said, "I was astonished! I had never heard or seen anything like it. This man jumped into the air, and sallied into the viola section, and did everything by memory, and without a baton. He was a magician, a wild man. The things that came out!"

The impression became indelible, and soon thereafter, when Bernstein met Mitropoulos, the conductor became equally impressed by Lenny's own musical gifts. He took the young man under his wing, allowed him to attend all his Boston rehearsals, became his mentor, and eventually told him that he must become a conductor—that conducting was his obvious calling.

"You know, it's very strange," Bernstein told me, "in my conducting I'm always compared to Koussevitzky or to Reiner. But nobody ever realizes how much of it is Dimitri —deep, deep—because it was the first conducting I ever really watched carefully, and listened to carefully."

If Mitropoulos' conducting influence helped to shape Bernstein's own style, of equal importance was Mitropoulos' relationship with the men of the orchestras he conducted—and particularly the men of the New York Philharmonic which Mitropoulos led from 1950 to 1957, and which became Bernstein's own orchestra the next year. It was a matter of love. Mitropoulos was anything but the tyrannical conductor of the Toscanini, Reiner, or even Koussevitzky variety. He loved the men individually and as a group, and while this ultimately proved something of a disadvantage, it was often reflected in the best of the performances he got out of them.

Lenny recalled many such performances, telling me that he couldn't believe what he was hearing, the feeling that waves of love were emanating from the orchestra to Mitropoulos and back. "They adored him. He knew everything so completely and he knew it so instinctually. He conveyed it so instinctually."

This reciprocal love between conductor and members of the orchestra is a Mitropoulos-inspired characteristic of Bernstein's own relationship with his orchestra—not because he emulates Mitropoulos, but because Bernstein's own nature and temperament are similar in

52

this respect, and because through Mitropoulos he saw that it was possible to be this kind of conductor.

Yet another Mitropoulos influence is apparent in repertory. The Greek conductor's performances of the Ravel Piano Concerto, in which he played the solo part as well, inspired Lenny to make the work virtually his own, conducting it from the keyboard as Mitropoulos did. The Schumann Second Symphony is another lifetime piece, first heard in a performance by Mitropoulos. Beethoven's C-Sharp Minor Quartet, played by all the strings of the orchestra, is still a Bernstein favorite, first heard when done by Mitropoulos.

And so it was Mitropoulos who first helped Lenny to become a conductor, who urged him to work with Reiner at Curtis, who sent a letter of recommendation to Koussevitzky when Lenny applied for admission to the conducting class of the just-opened Berkshire Music Center at Tanglewood. In short, it was Mitropoulos whose lean and awesome magnetism, whose apocalyptic musical vision and daring, excited and inspired the young Leonard Bernstein.

Fritz Reiner, while a major influence, did not create as much of an emotional impact on Lenny—not as compared with the effect of Mitropoulos and Koussevitzky on him. Still, Bernstein learned a tremendous amount from Reiner, who was tough and demanding. No standard was too high. He early imprinted on Lenny's mind the axiom that unless one really knew every last note of a score, one had no business standing on the podium in front of an orchestra. Lenny told me that Reiner was ruthless in his quizzing, that nothing was good enough, that no one was ever good enough. Bernstein nevertheless managed to become the *Liebling* of his class, much to the consternation of other Curtis students.

It was at Curtis that Bernstein first conducted an orchestra. While Fritz Reiner regularly directed the Institute's student orchestra, he occasionally allowed his students to have a try at it. Lenny describes his first conducting experience as unforgettable. "It was Brahms' Third, first movement," he told me. "I went mad! I was engulfed in a sea of sound! I was not prepared for this. It came at me with such rushes, and I was conducting like a mad, mad . . . like a dying swimmer in the ocean. Engulfed in a hurricane of sound! It's incredible the first time. No one can know what it's like to stand *in* an orchestra. I'm sure I was just horrible. But that was the first time for me."

In 1940, Leonard Bernstein applied for study at Tanglewood. Armed with letters of recommendation from Mitropoulos, Reiner, and Aaron Copland, he was accepted, and thus began his intense and beautiful friendship with Serge Koussevitzky.

"I was thinking only yesterday," Lenny tells me, "that this relationship lasted only eleven years. I was amazed, because I would have thought that it had occupied a much greater part of my life. This was 1940, and he died in '51. We were so close. We loved each other so! I think he, never having had a son, needed me as a son. And I needed him as a father. He always felt we looked alike. Many people remarked about that. Now even more, as I grow older. They say, 'Oh, I see Koussevitzky!' So there was also something mysterious and destined about that relationship."

Koussevitzky's was a continuing influence because the two men remained close for eleven consecutive years, whereas Bernstein saw Mitropoulos only sporadically. Koussevitzky was a dictatorial conductor and grand, one of the last of the great old school of European tyrants, but he was a very kind, warm, simple man underneath this. Bernstein recalls that Koussy would go into detail on how to approach the orchestra—how to come on stage, how to stand on the podium. He had been a friend of Stanislavsky's.

"I loved Koussy," says Bernstein. "I loved him enormously. I loved him mostly for his foibles, because when we were together he was not the *grand seigneur,* except when he was teaching me in the early days."

As a conductor, Bernstein is often compared to Koussevitzky. Lenny feels this is only part of the story. He considers the Mitropoulos, and even more, the Reiner influence as major elements in his development as a conductor.

"You see, people always see what they want to see, which is why they attack what they call the acrobatics, the big gestures, the dramatic leaps. What they don't see is the Reiner part of it, or the Koussevitzky part of it, which is very delicate and can be very small, and which, I'm sure is more than fifty per cent of the whole thing, maybe more than eighty per cent. They see only the big things."

Lenny pauses. The afternoon has drifted into early evening. Lenny picks up a pencil and plunges into one of his British puzzles. Suddenly he is totally engrossed. Cautiously he writes in a word. "This must be right. You know, people consult reference books when working on these puzzles, but I prefer not to. It somehow spoils it for me."

At this moment, little Nina comes to the door. She is carrying an empty Coke bottle. She has decided to throw it away, she says, and thinks that Lenny's studio has the appropriate basket for it. Actually, she wants to be with her Daddy. Lenny lays aside the puzzle and puts her in his lap. A cuddle-session ensues. Soon Jamie and Alexander are at the door. "Dinner is ready," says one of them. We all get up. Lenny puts his arms around Nina and Alexander. We all go in to dinner.

10.

A merry table this evening. Felicia looks radiant in a pretty Pucci dress. The food, as always, is delicious. Jamie and Alexander had been water-skiing that afternoon and their faces glow. Jamie had also been invited to explore the teen-age life of Porto Ercole, but found it depressing. "They don't talk about anything," she says. "They're a boring bunch." Alexander announces he has memorized all the titles and authors of a set of classics lining one entire shelf of the library. Lenny promptly quizzes him. Alexander gets them letter-perfect. "Now you might try reading them," Lenny tells him. "Later, Dad," says Alexander.

Talk now turns to Felicia's homeland. "Have you ever heard the Chilean national anthem?" she asks me. I hadn't, and urge her to sing it for us. "Yes, do sing it, Felicia," says Lenny. "Very well," she says, "but I warn you, it's very long!" Much giggling from the children, who have heard it before. Felicia, looking very solemn, and trying not to laugh, stands up. She embarks on the anthem. It is, indeed, very, very long. Felicia gets more and more inspired as the song progresses. She even sings the instrumental interludes, to which Lenny lends loud support. The anthem is endless. Everyone becomes quite hysterical with Felicia's performance. Finally Felicia collapses in her chair. Riotous laughter all around.

The talk turns from Chile to the Bernsteins' wedding day. Alexander wants details. So does Jamie. So do I. Nina wants another hug from Daddy.

FELICIA: The night before our wedding, my mother was there....

LENNY: Everybody was very keyed up. Nobody was quite sure that we should get married.

FELICIA: Shirley and Burtie decided to liven up the proceedings by going to one of those joke stores and buying up everything they could conceive of.

LENNY: It was B.B.'s idea. To make the occasion fun.

FELICIA: It was a hysterical night. There were cigarettes that when you smoked them made snow. Spoons that didn't spoon up anything. Finally I said, "I'm terribly sorry. I don't feel very well." I went upstairs, saying I had a headache, and asked for aspirin. And they brought me the aspirin with a tumbler of water, which I began to drink, but the water never came out of the glass. Another joke. It was the last straw. I wanted to fling it at them and say, "This is a houseful of loonies, madmen, monsters!" And their voices were very high and shrill and hysterical.

LENNY: Well, I told you, they were all very keyed up. Felicia was finally taken to where she was staying—the Ritz, in Boston. I was, of course, staying in the familial home.

FELICIA: Yes. He was really the bride!

LENNY: I was put to bed with something like twelve Seconals, trembling and screaming, with Burtie and Shirley holding a hand apiece and wet cloths on my forehead.

FELICIA: If we had been alone, we probably would have gotten quite drunk, and gotten married, and that would have been it. But such a thing was made of it.

LENNY: It was a small wedding, though.

FELICIA: No, it wasn't really. I said I would marry you in Boston because your family wished you to have a temple wedding. There were to have been exactly thirteen people.

LENNY: And that was how many came—the first two rows of the temple. That's all.

FELICIA: No, Lenny. There were thousands of people I had never before seen in my life.

LENNY: What? Thousands? Oh, come on!

FELICIA: Well, at the lunch. At your house.

LENNY: That was in the house, not at the temple.

FELICIA: That's right, but it all went around from the living room to the dining room, to the....

LENNY: No. At the lunch there were a dozen people.

FELICIA: No, no. Don't you remember?

LENNY: That was the reception, maybe, where people could come in and out.

FELICIA: Excuse me, excuse me, it was the lunch. It started in the dining room and it went that way, and that way into the hallway, into the living room. It kept going and going. It was a table that had no end.

LENNY: No. There were twelve people.

FELICIA: Ask Burtie.

LENNY: There was Abie and Annie and Rabbi Hochman....

FELICIA: And Rabbi Kazis and the Cantor, and people I'd never seen before.

LENNY: And you were seated next to my grandmother, that marvelous lady from Russia, with bright blue eyes. Of course, you couldn't communicate with her. It was a nightmare. And then you had to go through a conversion, in the morning, before the ceremony.

FELICIA: I had to sign a paper.

LENNY: And you had to speak lines from the Book of Ruth.

FELICIA: No, I just had to follow the....

LENNY: Bouncing Cantor? You had to say, "Whither thou goest I will go, and there will I be buried, and thy people shall be my people." You know.

FELICIA: And my mother, before I went off, crossed me.

LENNY: She crossed you off the list?

FELICIA: Lenny!

LENNY: Her mother had to stand with her at the conversion.

FELICIA: No! Are you crazy? My mother never knew I went through that! She was at the ceremony.

LENNY: Oh, yes. She kept her fingers crossed during the ceremony.

FELICIA: Yes, and I had to prop her up, poor thing. But she did behave marvelously.

LENNY: We came out of the ceremony, finally, white and trembling.

FELICIA: I was wearing a white short dress and yellow roses.

LENNY: Beautiful, she looked! Oh, God, she looked elegant. I, *invece*, was wearing Koussevitzky's white suit. He had died that June and the wedding was in September. Olga Koussevitzky gave me all of Koussy's clothes to be married in, including shoes, socks, a white suit, shirt, tie—the works. We were to have been married on his lawn at Tanglewood, but he died. And in order to carry out Olga's wishes I had to be married in his clothes. The day before the wedding I had that to contend with. I had to go to a local tailor, and have everything altered. It was a rush, and it didn't work out too well. I went nearly insane. The white shoes were cramping me and the pants were too big. But I had to look like Koussevitzky.

FELICIA: Yes. I married Koussevitzky!

LENNY: But the wedding was only a dozen people.

FELICIA: Ask Burtie.

New York apartment: Morning

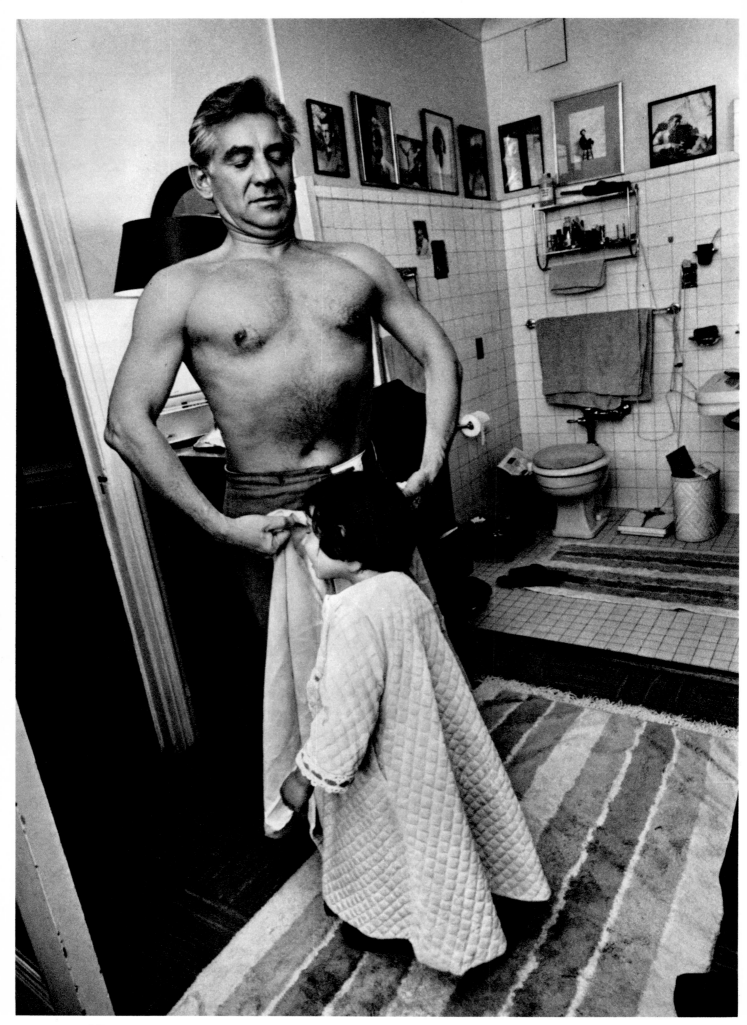

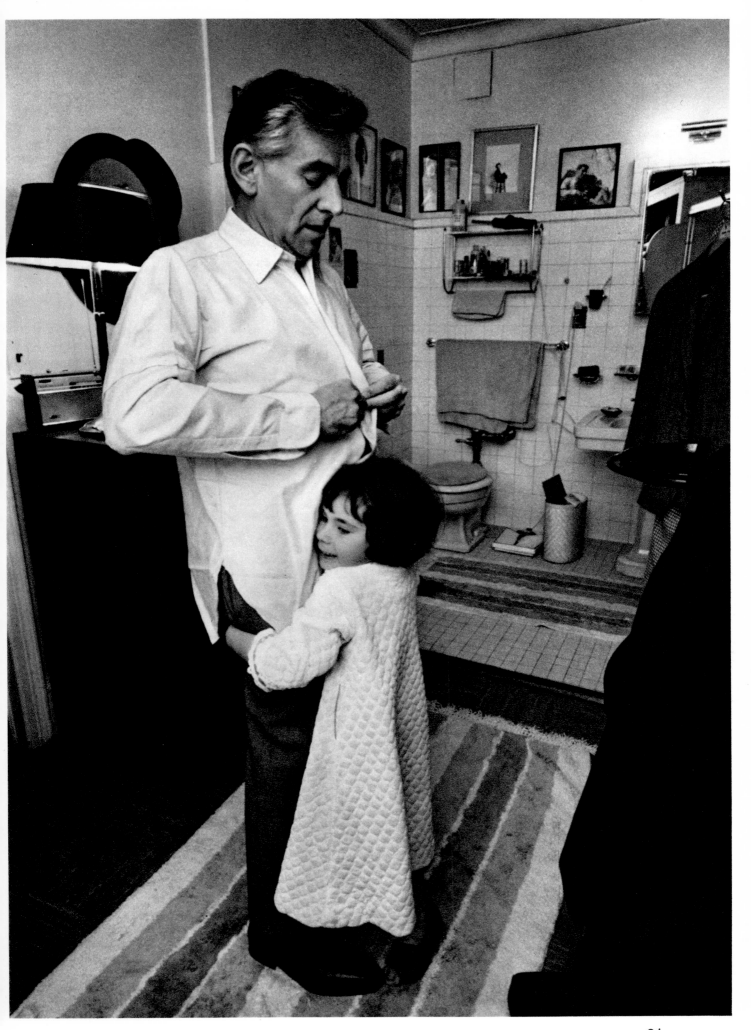

With Composer Lukas Foss (below); with Foss and Violinist Isaac Stern (opposite)

Playback: At recording sessions with John McClure, Columbia Records

11. "Let's go to Giglio!" says Alexander. "Yes, let's go to Giglio," cries Jamie. "I'm for Giglio," say I. "Then what are we waiting for?" says Lenny. "Let's all go to Giglio!"

We are back on Mrs. Thorne's beautiful sailboat. She too has agreed that Giglio, one of the islands clustering about Monte Argentario, is decidedly a place to visit. It is a mountain rising, almost tenderly, out of the Tyrrhenian. At its top stands a medieval city, miraculously intact, untouched by time or the calumnies of tourism.

On the sailboat, Lenny feels at one with himself. The water is calm and transparent. The boat glides smoothly toward Giglio. The trip takes a few hours and we all lie back on the comfortable cushions, allowing the sun and the breeze to turn all of us into idealized picture-postcard vacationers. To abet the near-cliché of the scene, one of the crewmen, a ruddy-faced Neapolitan with knowing eyes, begins singing the old Neapolitan songs—"Santa Lucia" and the like. Most of us wish he'd stop, but Lenny is enchanted. He wants to hear more, and makes him sing all his songs.

When the singing finally comes to an end, everyone falls into one of those incredibly suspended silences. Each is with his own thoughts, yet very much with one another. Not a cloud in the sky, and a sense of well-being shared by everyone. A splendid moment!

I look at Lenny. There is still so much I want to know. Could this be the moment to ask him to recount the events of his Philharmonic debut? Probably not. His thoughts don't seem to dwell on the past just now. Perhaps with all that crewman's singing, I could ask him about his own vocal output, not his theater songs, but his concert songs. I recalled listening to his cycle *I Hate Music,* and remembered how Jennie Tourel sang it at her own debut recital in New York in 1943. Besides, Lenny had just written three new songs here in Ansedonia. Why not? I'd try it.

"Ah, my songs," says Lenny. "Actually, Jennie sang those songs quite a few months before she sang them at her Town Hall debut in New York. In fact, they have a great deal to do with that famous debut you keep wanting me to talk about." In the summer of 1943, Koussevitzky had asked Jennie Tourel to give a recital at the Lenox Library, and he asked Bernstein to accompany her. "I remember going to Jennie's apartment on 81st Street and Broadway, in one of those musical hotels, and I found this rather gypsyish, wonderful woman. She tells me now that I appeared in an outlandish outfit and she remembers my being very outspoken. At one point she asked me if I had written any songs. According to her recollection I said, 'Oh, I've written some, but I'm afraid you couldn't sing them because of your accent.' I was a rude little bastard. Anyway, I had brought them and she sang them, and she sang them marvelously. I said, 'To hell with the accent. You sound just glorious.' She decided to include my songs in her Lenox recital as a birthday present to me on that fateful twenty-fifth of August, and repeated them in her debut recital at Town Hall on the fateful fourteenth of November following. So, you see, Jennie's somehow bound up with my destiny."

Indeed, this meeting between Leonard Bernstein and Jennie Tourel based, as it was, on a musical collaboration resulted in a friendship that has spanned twenty-five years. Miss Tourel, whose own career in opera and on the concert stage has proved both durable and singular, became a key collaborator, not only in Bernstein's own music (the *Jeremiah* Symphony and *Kaddish*), but in works of Mahler, Ravel, Mussorgsky, and others performed with Bernstein conducting or accompanying on the piano. In fact, this very summer, when Bernstein conducted the Israel Philharmonic on Mount Scopus, found Jennie Tourel the soloist in Mahler's Second Symphony.

"There's Giglio," Mrs. Thorne breaks in to say. And a small sand beach at the foot of the island comes into view. As we approach it, everyone decides to swim toward the beach. Lenny is the first to plunge into the water. He and Alexander are the first to reach shore. They wave to us and go off exploring. After a few minutes they are back in the water, swimming near and into a huge grotto. They return with hands full of sea urchins. We cut them in half and suck out their contents. Delicious. A delicate, salty taste. Lenny comments on their extraordinary color and texture.

But an extraordinary lunch is also being prepared aboard the sailboat. Soon we are feasting on a large assortment of shellfish, cheeses, cold cuts, and salads. And as the boat makes ready to sail into the island's tiny port, and the day moves into an intense early afternoon heat, we lie somewhat sleepily awaiting the ancient marvel that is Giglio.

We take a taxi to the top of the mountain. A walled city—a medieval Saracen fortress city, complete with turrets and bastions! An amazing sight. And inhabited by a population seemingly unaware of the historical setting in which it lives and works. We walk along the narrowest, most crooked of streets. It is also a climactic city, in that it rises by way of circuitous routes toward a twelfth-century castle, the city's apex.

Lenny, Alexander, and Jamie lead the way and move quickly. They fly up and down ancient stairs. Alexander balances on a ruined wall. Old villagers walk past, hardly noticing their exhilaration. The rest of us follow more slowly. The sudden, precipitous views of the sea and island below are breathtaking and dizzying. We observe Lenny admiring an odd

irregularity along a thickset wall, the cracks near a stone-framed window. He finds a plaque pounded into the wall—a dedication to a deceased army-band conductor. Lenny studies it carefully. The city atop Giglio is very small. One circles it in a matter of minutes. Soon we make the descent in the taxi, quickly reaching the port. We decide to have something to drink and sit down at an outdoor café.

Were this New York, London, Vienna, Rome, or Paris, Leonard Bernstein, sitting with his family in an open-air café, would immediately cause excitement. He would be recognized, approached, and treated as the celebrity he is. Here in tiny Giglio probably no one has heard of Leonard Bernstein and Lenny is delighted. While he often enjoys and even welcomes the fuss and adulation his presence causes, he is relieved by the anonymity that has, in fact, extended throughout most of his Italian summer.

It was interesting to observe Bernstein's gregariousness despite his anonymity. He involved himself in conversations with the fishermen on the quays, with shopkeepers, with townspeople. And Lenny's Italian, while not fluent, is quite good, and helped in the cause of making him new friends.

When Lenny was recognized, which was mainly by the vacationers of Porto Ercole, Porto Santo Stefano, and Ansedonia, that electric something took hold of them and that feeling of being in the presence of a star consistently worked its magic. But then a sense of awe, mingled with embarrassment, and a kind of fake nonchalance as well as genuine pleasure, attends those who come into close proximity to Bernstein. Standing in a New York theater lobby with Bernstein or just walking down the street with him produces this effect. Some people simply come up and offer their compliments, others call him Lenny and ask for his autograph, still others nudge each other and whisper, "That's Leonard Bernstein!" Lenny is usually responsive and, when approached, will always have a few kind words. But here, in Giglio, this does not happen. We sit amid Italians enjoying an afternoon drink and then amble back to the boat for the journey home.

The colors of the day have changed. Huge billowing clouds drift slowly above a still calm sea. Slowly we move out of port, and soon sea, air, and sky again make all of us recede into our private thoughts. But I don't wish the lengthy journey home to go by without some more talk with Lenny.

"Didn't Artur Rodzinski die in Italy?" I ask him. Lenny looks up at me. His lynx-gray eyes regard me wearily. "Oh, God, are we back to ancient history? Yes, Artur Rodzinski died of a heart attack here in Italy. That was after his period with the Chicago Symphony, the post he held after the New York Philharmonic."

"How did you come to be his assistant conductor at the Philharmonic?"

"Well, you won't believe this, but it was strictly according to God's instructions. At least, that's what Rodzinski told me. You see, he was an Oxford Grouper—a Buchmanite—and consulted God in prayer two or three times a day. The story becomes even more compelling when you think that Rodzinski and I had never met. And that this invitation was tendered me on my birthday, that unforgettable twenty-fifth of August, 1943!"

Lenny had felt on top of the world. He was newly twenty-five, which in the conducting world meant being little more than a child. He was making $125 a week. He moved into a room in Carnegie Hall. His job was to be ready at any moment to take over a rehearsal or a concert if the conductor or the guest conductor were indisposed. He had to attend all rehearsals. He had to be on hand.

Indeed, to be an assistant conductor in those days meant keeping to an incredible schedule, and it was a post usually open only to the very few, the very gifted, and the very lucky. Today, chances for a young conductor to be made assistant conductor of a large symphony orchestra have increased enormously. Bernstein is entirely responsible. Very early on, as music director of the New York Philharmonic, he instigated a policy of hiring three assistant conductors—chosen from all parts of the world—for each Philharmonic season. The assistants have been selected by a jury of internationally known conductors in a competition held each year in New York City. Appropriately named the Dimitri Mitropoulos Competition for Conducting, it is ably sponsored by the Federation of Jewish Philanthropies and supported by funds from the Leonard Bernstein Foundation and the New York Philharmonic. Bernstein has thus opened the way for professional talent to show and practice its skill under the best possible circumstances. Once their tenure with the Philharmonic is over, these young men and women are usually hired by orchestras here or abroad. In short, to be a professional conductor is today no longer a matter of waiting out the years, of being burdened by the awesome traditions that have been the eternal points of reference of most aspiring conductors.

But in 1943 Bernstein was among the very few chosen, and, according to Rodzinski, chosen by God himself. Rodzinski, being a member of the Oxford Group, was given to proselytizing. He would describe the wonder of losing the ego and how this had made a new man of him. And that Lenny should follow suit. All was shadows. It seemed to be just Rodzinski and God. The ego, not to say people, just disappeared.

84

"I didn't like that very much, because I always thought people were more important even than God. That's how I see God, anyway —in his creations and manifestations," says Lenny.

Obviously, Rodzinski was a complicated man, the kind of man Bernstein would have to treat with a certain care and caution. Be that as it may, Lenny embarked on his duties with characteristic enthusiasm. He began to learn a great deal, and to know intimately the orchestra of which he was one day to be musical director.

"Rodzinski was really a remarkable conductor," Bernstein told me. "He had a great flair for conducting. He was dramatic, fairly imitative. He had studied a lot of Koussevitzky's performances. He secretly and privately confessed a great disrespect for Koussevitzky, but he imitated his Russian music.

"But he had authority and power and a fine ear for sonority. And the men respected him. I was very pleased to be in attendance at all these rehearsals, never thinking for a moment that anything would ever occur in my favor. He would ask me, now and then, to conduct the orchestra so he could walk around Carnegie Hall and test the acoustics. He would try shifting the orchestra's seating, putting carpets down or drapes up. Doing everything we now do at Philharmonic Hall. He was not happy with the acoustics at Carnegie Hall, which have been greatly overvalued, I think. (It's gotten better since they rebuilt the stage, but it's always been a freak hall. If you move from one place to another it's like changing halls.)

"In any case, I learned a great deal about acoustics and orchestra handling and sound. I admired very much the thoroughness with which Rodzinski rehearsed. I also saw mistakes he made, both in psychological relations with the men and through his own particular foibles. But he was always very nice to me and would invite me to his apartment for tea, and talk to me again about the Oxford Group, and how I should join it—because 'All of us artists have tremendous egos. They get in our way and we must give ourselves to God.' But he hadn't convinced me at all."

Still, Bernstein was enjoying it all very much. Rodzinski allowed him on the podium to conduct readings of new pieces that came his way, because, as Lenny recalled, he felt he couldn't really judge a new score by eye; he could judge better by listening. So Bernstein received several opportunities to read with the orchestra. He stood on the podium and got to know the men better, and he and the men became friends.

"And one day," says Lenny, "Bruno Walter got sick—"

"We're home!" cries Mrs. Thorne.

A slight rage wells up in me, as the much-hoped-for debut story was about to be recounted. It has been stopped once more by whatever uncooperative guardian angel protects Lenny from having to tell it. He, of course, is delighted, and taps me on the back consolingly as we make our way back toward our separate villas.

2.

A hot, hot day. Cicadas on everyone's nerves. No breeze. Everyone feels slightly desperate. Jamie sudenly feels like singing Schumann's *Die Mondnacht*. Lenny agrees to accompany her. In halting German, Jamie begins. She runs through the song. Lenny now makes her sing it again, explaining how it should be interpreted. He sings along with her. Jamie gives up. Gets a book and sits on the terrace. Alexander wants to go swimming. Lenny declines.

They had been swimming that morning near and into several grottos. "Remember the creature in the grotto?" says Alexander. "Tell John about the creature, Daddy." Lenny says, "Ah, yes. In that incredible violet grotto, Alexander and I have fathomed a creature. It is a creature that does not speak but communicates, that is invisible but present, that soothes the soul, lifts the spirit, entrances the mind." He punctuates the speech with a chord on the piano.

Now *I* feel like singing Schumann's *Die Mondnacht*. Lenny obliges by accompanying me. I sing it badly—not being a singer—but he has kind words for my interpretation. Now we again decide to play a Mozart four-hand piano sonata. As always, playing with Lenny puts me on my toes. He's too good, I'm too terrible. But we manage to finish together. Lenny hums along, points out the gorgeous passages, emphasizes this or that section in the sonata. I learn a great deal about Mozart, four-hands.

The heat gets oppressive. Felicia is taking a nap. Nina is taking a nap. I sense everyone is about to take a nap and I feel the time might be spent doing something else—like...something funny...like....Why not? A mock radio broadcast on the tape recorder. I suggest it to Lenny. Jamie and Alexander are game. They urge Lenny to join in. I will act as announcer for a worldwide broadcast of a play called *The Private World of Leonard Bernstein*. Suddenly, we're all huddled around the machine. A silly project, but spirits are lifting. We decide to do the tape in one of the shaded arbors near Lenny's studio. It's cooler there. Alexander sits on Lenny's knee, Jamie draws up a chair. We sit in a circle. I turn on the recorder. An embarrassed silence. Everyone bursts out laughing. I introduce the program. Lenny is at his self-mocking best. There is much mugging. His voice is exaggeratedly actorish. It all starts with great hilarity.

THE PRIVATE WORLD OF LEONARD BERNSTEIN

A Farce That Ends in Truth
Starring: LEONARD BERNSTEIN as LEONARD BERNSTEIN
JAMIE BERNSTEIN as JAMIE BERNSTEIN
ALEXANDER BERNSTEIN as ALEXANDER BERNSTEIN
And Introducing: JOHN GRUEN as THE HOST

ACT I

THE HOST: Presenting, The Private World of Leonard Bernstein, a private glimpse into a world-renowned family.

LENNY: This is the glamorous, world-famous, wildly fascinating, mysterious, hard-to-approach Leonard Bernstein. Think of it. You are listening to his very own voice at this moment. Only think! The sounds you are hearing issue from the throat, the tender, golden throat of what is certainly the greatest conductor of his time, what will certainly turn out to be the greatest composer of his time. A charming social figure. A lovable family man. An expert aquatic performer. A skier, horseback-rider, and loafer! This is he, friends. Yes, this is *he*. At this very moment. Can you imagine it? I put my lips together: Mmmmm. Take them apart: Aaaaa. Can you see these very lips in your mind's eye? Mmmmmm—coming through my Roman nose. That nose you dream about at night. I have on my right and left two of my twenty adorable children. These being the sixth and seventeenth. Jamie and Alexander. Ah, Jamie and Alexander! The children all of you wish *you* had. Perfect, beautiful, well-mannered, intelligent, humor-

JAMIE: ous, obedient. Perhaps, Jamie, you would like to introduce yourself.

JAMIE: This is the famed, envied Jamie Bernstein, who as you know is the daughter of the famed, envied Leonard Bernstein, who as you know is the son of the not very much envied Samuel J. Bernstein. I find myself much privileged to be the daughter of this famed and marvelous father that I have, who is now looking at me with the greatest of hairy eyeballs. I have been asked to talk a little about Dad. Dad is a swell guy. He's real cool. When I go out on my dates and come home at one in the morning, Dad doesn't yell. Dad doesn't get mad. He just takes me into his studio, gives me a long hard glance, and says, "Don't do it again, son!" Then I know that everything is all right. You see, there are so many of us kids that he gets confused every now and then, especially since my name is Jamie!

And my brother Alice, here on my right, also has his problems. You remember the famous lines from *West Side Story,* "My sister wears a mustache, my brother wears a dress." Well, here it is. Alexander, your dress is beautiful today. May I describe it for you? My brother is a swell gal. He has this little white dress with purple flowers on it that start at the neck and go all over the place. I think it's the most beautiful thing! Alice, would you like to say a couple of words?

ALEXANDER: Well, hi, man! My Dad is such a square. I mean, he won't even give me the Maserati! Anyway, Jamie, your mustache needs more waxing.

LENNY: Tell us something of what your life is like.

ALEXANDER: My life. My family life—oh, oh! I was sent to the hardest school in New York. I have to work, work, work! My father is a very swell man. And though swell, he's square. Very square. He doesn't understand us kids. He just doesn't get it. For example, in Vail, Colorado, one night we went to the Casino Vail. My father pushed my sister onto the dancing floor. They were playing the music from *Zorba the Greek,* and my father wanted to dance outside the ring of people who were jumping about, and my sister absolutely refused. But finally they edged to the circle, and my father edged her into the middle of the circle. And my father got down on his knees, and bent backwards, and started swinging a handkerchief around her. And Jamie, just not to be a fink, to be the little cutie that she is, danced with him and took the handkerchief. Finally, at the end of the dance, everybody was yelling. Jamie hid behind the piano and everybody was trying to get her autograph because of that great Greek dance that they had danced. Jamie said she had never been so embarrassed in her life. But, now, back to my wonderful father.

LENNY: This is that wildly famous, mysterious, fascinating, envied Leonard Bernstein—envied and somewhat castrated at the moment by the tale that's just been told. You see, my dear friends, I don't know many of

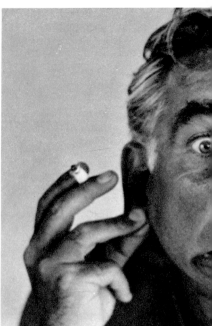

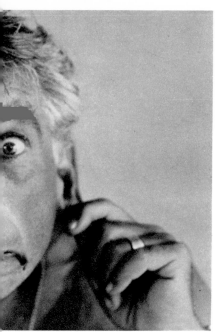
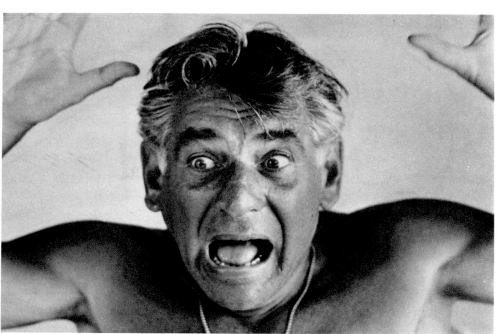

you. I don't know many people. It's very hard for people to get to know me. But, still, I feel you're all my friends, at least for the duration of this program, because we're very close through this extraordinary medium of communication which is our century's gift to us. And so I say, my friends, my *dear* friends, you may have garnered the impression from my children that they are critical little beasts—ugly little carpers, who delight in nothing so much as in tearing their revered father to bits. Weli, it's all true. That's just what they are! God damn it, I'm leaving this house and never coming back! I'm not appreciated. *(Sobbing.)* I can't bear it anymore! All they do is hammer, hammer, hammer!

JAMIE: You want your white suit or your black suit? You want your hairspray?

LENNY: All right, Jamie. You'll go to your room and not come out till after dinner. Good-bye.

ALEXANDER: Little does he know that Jamie has a secret exit!

LENNY: And you, Alexander, will sit on the top of this table and write five hundred times: "I will never again malign my father." Oh, God! What a dreary family we are!

(Curtain)

HOST: Act I of The Private World of Leonard Bernstein has just been heard by you millions of people—an intimate glimpse into a world-renowned family! Was it not moving? Was it not extraordinary? Was it not something to remember?

(Music: Tchaikovsky's Piano Concerto No. 1)

HOST: We come now to Act II of The Private World of Leonard Bernstein. And we hand the microphone back to the celebrated maestro.

ACT II

(All three are singing the round "Non Nobis Domine," the maestro singing consistently off pitch. The round ends in shambles. They then sing the round "Follow, Follow." It goes better.)

LENNY: All right, Alexander, did you bring home that pot last night? No? How many times must I tell you? I gave you the money! What did you do with it?

ALEXANDER: Mike didn't have it.

LENNY: Jamie? What about you? Did you have any luck?

JAMIE: Potluck?

LENNY: You know what my whole trouble is about singing in tune? I have no breath. I run out of breath so fast that after a note I force. But back to us, and "Whither Youth?" When I was a youth, I was always looking for ways of breaking rules and being very different from my parents—being as different as possible from my parents, in fact. But I didn't succeed very well.

JAMIE: I think you did okay. You're not too much like Grandpa.

LENNY: No, I know. I *have* broken away a lot. And I succeeded in ways that were positive, which were useful. Music being one of them. But I'm so like him in many ways—God, I'm terribly like him. I see that already in you. But the point is all young people try to turn away from their parents. As much as they love them.

JAMIE: As much as they also try to copy them.

LENNY: Yes. And that, in spite of that, there are certain things which are deeply ingrained, and you just can't get rid of them. What are all of the things in yourself, Jamie, that remind you of me?

JAMIE: Oh, lots of things.

LENNY: You mean things that you reject and resent?

JAMIE: Things that I resent, but find myself doing also. It's a very odd mixture. Such things as interrupting.

LENNY: Oh, I don't ever interrupt!

(Much clearing of throats by children.)

Except I just interrupted you. My big problem is resentment at *being* interrupted. Anyway, go on.

JAMIE: Other things are: I'm short-tempered.

LENNY: Am I short-tempered?

JAMIE: No.

LENNY: I'm not. I have enormous patience, as a matter of fact. How often have you seen me lose my temper? I mean you can really count them on the fingers of one hand, can't you?

JAMIE: Yes. But then again, you don't have that much to lose your temper about.

LENNY: Oh, I don't know!

JAMIE: Anyway, it's hard to explain. If you don't have the great *goal*. I mean, when you're in sort of an economic rut, when you find yourself in a strange place in society, and you can't get out of it....

LENNY: I know whom you're thinking of.

JAMIE: Who? No, you don't know whom I'm thinking of.

LENNY: Well, I know whom *I'm* thinking of and it fits what you're saying. But

go ahead.

JAMIE: Anyway, you get that sort of feeling of nothingness—frustration. No, not even frustration—just nowhere to go. And a constant feeling of strain and aimlessness, and it all leads to....

LENNY: Temper tantrums?

JAMIE: Not tantrums. Just temper.

LENNY: But one suffers from not letting it out, too. I mean, I think I pay a certain penalty for not having a quick temper, for keeping it all bottled up. But then, luckily, I have other outlets, like conducting. Because you can vent a great deal of rage during the course of a Beethoven symphony.

JAMIE: Yes, it must be marvelous to conduct, and rant and rage and know that you can get away with it. It must be a great feeling.

LENNY: Well, it's not the jumping around. I'm talking about the musical experience. You're seeing it as an exterior, visual thing on the podium. You see, I forget I'm in public when I'm *in* the music. But the actual rage expression of Beethoven himself is something that you not only identify with, but you take on. It becomes *your* expression, and at the end of it you're purged in some way. Don't you think so, Alexander? Alexander is not short-tempered either. What he is, is oversensitive.

ALEXANDER: Yes. Emotional.

LENNY: Well, we're all that. No. I think your problem is that you're *so* easily hurt, or you feel easily rejected, left out, and the tears are ever-ready, just lurking behind the hairy eyeball. They come flowing out.

ALEXANDER: No. It's not temper. Because temper is something that gets you aggravated by somebody else. No. It's myself.

JAMIE: How about when you're playing cards? That's a perfect example. Now that's not a question of somebody attacking you. We're just playing cards, say, and you lose....

LENNY: You're talking about competitiveness. Alexander is competitive. Therefore, his partner is his opponent, and his opponent is a rival **and, therefore,** it's somebody who's attacking him. If he doesn't win, he has been attacked and defeated. Right? And cards are a kind of symbol for that in life.

JAMIE: Consequently, Alexander loses his temper. Gets furious. Throws cards. Runs around. And sometimes we fight physically as well.

LENNY: Good lord!

JAMIE: Oh, yes!

LENNY: I guess I *have* seen that once or twice —and long ago. But you tell it, Alexander. Let's have it from the horsey's mouth.

ALEXANDER: Well, it has something to do with the other person, too. I mean, I'm not just trying to blame Jamie, but, I mean, if I lose—if I lose a card game, I won't just get up and hit her. I mean....

(Alexander is in tears)

HOST: The end of Act II. A dramatic story, wouldn't you say? As you may have gathered, there are many things that this renowned father and public figure does not know—but at all—about his children. And so this provocative, marvelous moment you are sharing is as much a revelation to Mr. Bernstein as it must be to you. Ah, well.... But—anyway—we now move you into Act III of TPWOLB.

ACT III

LENNY: This is all very interesting. Alexander, you were in a difficult moment just now because you were feeling accused of something, and you felt defensive, and you had to fight against it, and you felt it was an unjust accusation. What you were trying to say was that it's not all one-sided. That, somehow, you feel that when you lose a card game you are being taunted about losing it. It's being flaunted at you.

ALEXANDER: Well, Jamie and I don't ever finish a card game—and that proves it isn't really the losing. I haven't lost *yet*.

LENNY: But then, why did you fling the cards across the room?

ALEXANDER: Well, because she may have done something that hits a nerve, snaps a bell.

LENNY: What sort of thing?

ALEXANDER: Well, she teases me.

LENNY: Is your teasing threshold so low that you can't take much of it?

ALEXANDER: Yes, it's very low.

LENNY: Well then, that has something to do with criticism, doesn't it? That means you can't stand criticism very well. Right?

ALEXANDER: Well, I suppose I could. But at this age....

LENNY: But I'm talking about this age. What other age are you?

ALEXANDER: As of now, I have a very low tolerance of criticism.

LENNY: So what we have elicited so far is a

tendency on Jamie's part to be critical, and teasing, and gloating…and a little bit cruel, which she might very well deny. Or she might accept it with modifications. And a tendency on your part not to be able to stand it. Do both of these qualities of character seem to be inherited, or imitated, or in some way reflective of qualities in me? That's what we started out with, inherited qualities.

ALEXANDER: First of all, you can take criticism very well.

LENNY: You think I can?

JAMIE: Well, you've been given so much praise that you can afford to take a little criticism.

ALEXANDER: I mean, you can stand up to it, you can start yelling. But it won't really have an effect on you.

LENNY: Have you ever seen me *really* upset by newspaper criticism?

ALEXANDER: Yes. A few times.

LENNY: Really? It seems to me that at times I seem to react rather emotionally, resentfully. But it doesn't last very long. I can get into a state at breakfast, reading the papers and say, "I've got to do something about this," or "Now, they've gone too far," or "I've got to get someone to write a letter. Maybe fifty of my friends should get together and sign fifty signatures…."

JAMIE: Saying that you're great?

LENNY: No! Saying, "This is unjust. Personal opinion is one thing but misstatement of fact is another." But by the time I get to Philharmonic Hall for a rehearsal, intending to speak very seriously to somebody, I'll have forgotten the whole thing. It's kind of worn off. But I suppose I can be sensitive to criticism.

ALEXANDER: Also it can have an effect on you. You may not remember it. A long-lasting effect.

LENNY: Yes. Maybe because fifty friends didn't of their own accord spontaneously leap to my defense and sign such a letter! Do you agree to all this, Jamie?

JAMIE: To a certain extent. I find that the amount of criticism you can take is pretty good. I'm not just talking about newspaper criticism. That's about your work. I was thinking more about you, yourself.

LENNY: You mean from my near and dear ones?

JAMIE: From your near and dear ones. Like your driving. Now, for years and years we've all made cracks about your driving, and we all get scared and say, "We're never going to drive with Daddy again." But at one point this summer, there was a little straw that broke your camel's bad back. There was suddenly a point you couldn't take it anymore. You didn't blow up, or anything. But I could tell, and Mummy could, too.

LENNY: Without seeming to interrupt, may I say a little something right here? In our family there is a tradition of teasing that comes from my brother and sister. This is common among siblings, but I think it's wildly exaggerated among us three siblings because we're particularly close. The closer you are, the more you can get away with because you know it's not going to have any disastrous effects. And this has filtered down into *this* family. Also, Mummy is fond of a kind of intimate, loving, teasing criticism. I suppose that comes from her early life with *her* siblings. It has always been a sort of duty, sworn on oath, by all the members of all my family, to act as bringer-downers, so that Daddy doesn't go off on Cloud 9 with a wildly swelled head. It's a kind of protective thing—and I love it. Because I feel that it's done out of love and out of protectiveness. Especially on Mummy's side, I know that's true. I am constantly being brought down. I'm not complaining about this, just describing it. Daddy's fat belly when he was doing a Greek dance, Daddy's this and Daddy's that. This is part of every conversation, every day. Right? Daddy's driving. Daddy's reaction to something. Daddy's wrong jacket that he put on.

JAMIE: That last one got you pretty upset.

LENNY: Yes, that got me upset for a minute. I was more upset than I should have been. I don't know why. But you must also admit that Mummy goes somewhat overboard in that department. Mummy is perhaps the most critical single person I've ever met in my whole life. It's a wonderful thing to be, but you have to get used to it, and you have to know that it's not done in bad faith. I don't know what I would do without it, as a matter of fact. Because it is part of the expression of affection and protectiveness. I think it's like an unconsciously undertaken duty to keep Daddy down to earth. I mean, Burtie coming backstage. It's never, "Oh Lenny! How marvelous!" It's, "So, what's new? Nice place you've got here. Like what you've done with the walls." Or, after *Feste Romane*: "Respighi, or forever hold your peace!" There is a tradition of not coming in and bending the knee.

JAMIE: But I'm sure that's true of any family where someone is a conductor.

LENNY: No, it isn't. You should see Green Rooms of other conductors with *their* wives, and friends—and children. There the artist returns to the Green Room and there's a weeping, salivating group of adorers, including family and nonfamily. You can imagine what Toscanini's Green Room was like—I mean, he would come back from the podium and it was... High Mass. But with my two siblings, when we haven't seen each other in a long time, instead of rushing into each other's arms—which we feel like doing, by the way—we'll be very casual, light a cigarette, and say, "I read a funny thing the other day." All before we say, "Hello." It's an old thing we have. But when, for example, Mummy comes backstage, and says, "Oh, that was something marvelous," then I know it *really* was. This makes it selective, and special, and not just that weekly or daily Mass that is celebrated in front of the altar of Toscanini, or whoever. I think it's a good thing and I'm not the worse for wear as a result of it.

A VOICE: Tea is served!

LENNY: Thank God.

13. Having watched Felicia Bernstein all summer long paint one portrait after another—of her children, of Adolph Green, of the gardener's grandson, I brazenly ask her to paint mine. Felicia, who tends to minimize every one of her many talents, protests, saying that she would probably be unable to do me justice. Discarding the ugly notion that Felicia might quite justifiably not feel like painting me, I persist in my request. I assume several outlandish poses. She bursts out laughing and finally gives in.

The small easel is set up in the villa's enclosed garden and Felicia carefully arranges her tubes of color, gets out her can of turpentine, her brushes, her paint rags. She and I are alone this afternoon. Lenny and the children have gone to visit Burtie and his wife and their children in Porto Ercole.

I sit posing, a drink and cigarettes at my side. I look at Felicia. Felicia looks at me. She studies my features. She rearranges my pose. Her face assumes a look of concentration. Her soft, hazel eyes are very discerning at this moment. Her face is a combination of delicacy and alertness. It reflects an innate elegance and an alert sensibility. In general, Felicia gives the simultaneous effect of composure and vivacity. Her movements have the quality of elation; these may not always reflect her mood, but they are intrinsic to her general mien. She is a tiny woman whose size is deceptive because of the refinement of her proportions.

She begins to paint me. Within, the cook, the maid, and the maid's husband are heard chattering—far from quietly—in a torrent of Italian. They are in the kitchen, preparing this evening's meal. Felicia and I are amused by the nonstop jabber. Her eyes dart from me to the easel. She applies careful strokes to the painting.

When Felicia is at her easel, she does not talk. She paints. Throughout the summer, Felicia Montealegre Bernstein has been slightly restive. She had not anticipated the heat to be quite so intense. Too, the sun produced a mild, though annoying rash on her legs, which did not seem to go away. This, added to Lenny's aggravated back problem, contrived to make Felicia's summer in Ansedonia somewhat less than perfect. Still, there were excursions to Rome and Florence, good times with Lenny and the children, visits from good friends, the sea and pool to compensate for some of these negative feelings.

Felicia is not easy to get to know. She is a private person. She is guarded. She feels that something of her life will be lost if it is made public. Felicia does not enjoy Lenny's non-privacy. She resents strangers who refer to him as Lenny. The household word that is Leonard Bernstein almost makes her shudder. Yet to people who know her well Felicia is irresistibly outgoing. Felicia alone and Felicia with Lenny are two distinctly different personalities. Alone she is very much her own person. Her sense of deft understatement gives her the individuality and separateness that constitute the great difference of temperament between herself and Lenny.

Felicia alone is a person passionately involved in helping causes she believes in, an avid reader of books on many subjects. She is a highly visual person whose love for art has prompted her to sculpt and study painting. Her sculptures—usually heads of her children—have great presence, delicacy, and immediacy. Her paintings reflect a genuine love for the properties of paint and its application in a manner that is always personal, always felt. Her still lifes and portraits emerge as sensitive yet direct expressions of her feelings. Painted in a more or less traditional vein, they disclose something of the private Felicia: her sense of

subtlety, inwardness, her imaginativeness.

She is, of course, enormously musical; it was her first tie with Lenny. Having studied the piano for many years, having been exposed to music all her life, she has developed a second sense in all things musical. She is both an intuitive and experienced musician. Bernstein values her opinions and seems continually to discover new insights when music is discussed between them.

But music was not to be her career. Her sense of perfection may have been the deterrent. Instead, for years Felicia Montealegre worked successfully as a stage and television actress. Her name, in fact, means a great deal to the rising generation of worshippers of TV dramatic stars of the 1950's. Again, however, Felicia tends to disparage her acting talents. Later in 1967, nevertheless, she was to be persuaded by director Mike Nichols to resume her career, as Birdie in the Broadway revival of *The Little Foxes*, by Lillian Hellman. Her portrayal of the unhappy Birdie made clear her very definite gifts as an actress, and the performance was as instinctual as it was un-hackneyed. She gave the role an intelligence it could easily lack and imbued the character with the sort of self-possession and secret fortitude that other actresses overlooked in their emphasis of its pitiable aspects.

During her years off the dramatic stage, Felicia performed as soloist in major symphonic works requiring the spoken or intoned word. Here again an inner strength, as well as a clear and beautiful speaking voice, made her performances authoritative and telling.

"Lenny has always been happy about my acting. It would be very easy for me to say, 'Well, look, I'm married to somebody who is so unbelievably talented—what can *I* do?' Or that I gave up my career to help my husband. But that's all nonsense. Lenny never demanded that I give up anything. I just did it."

Felicia with Lenny is yet another person. For one thing, she is not the typical conductor's wife, the kind who is always "there," who packs the bags and does all. In Bernstein's public life, she is more his friend in the background. And yet she is there for him. There is probably no one he can talk to as easily as he can to Felicia. She has a great capacity for looking at things objectively—and there is very little he does not tell her.

When Lenny tours and Felicia is along, she is part of everything. As the wife of Leonard Bernstein she is accorded every consideration and she responds with enthusiasm, good humor, and intelligence. Official dinners, private parties—functions she does not especially enjoy—find her nevertheless in splendid spirits and always totally charming. As a couple the Bernsteins are extraordinarily handsome. Felicia's taste in clothes is superb. With it all, Felicia is not given to taking the "social thing" very seriously. The Bernsteins are not part of the jet set, and "society" leaves them cold.

"The celebrated friends one meets only because one is oneself celebrated don't really count very much in your life. Those are not really what one would call friends. It lends color to life. It was fun (and actually very moving) to be asked to dinner with the Kennedys in the White House, and it is fun to go to the palace in Monaco and have a quiet dinner with Princess Grace and Prince Rainier. But it's like a set—like a playlet—and it doesn't ultimately mean much in your life," says Felicia Bernstein.

As for the private life between them, it is based on love and great mutual respect. "Lenny is so damned attractive. It's really the reason everybody loves him," Felicia tells me. "He has an unerring instinct for the shared life and he's a marvelous father. He has a much better 'nose' for what the children are all about

than I have. He's such a gamester. He can be happy for hours playing with the children. He has terrific patience. Also, Lenny is unlike the old-fashioned idea of a conductor. I mean, he is a musician and a man of the world. He's unbelievably well-read. He's a thinker. He's a man with an enormous variety of interests. And he likes people who have that too. That's why we don't tend to have just musical friends." She lapsed into silence for an hour or more.

"There! I think it's finished," exclaims Felicia. The light in the villa's enclosed garden is diminishing. I feel quite stiff from sitting still in one position. Felicia has been painting steadily and with enormous concentration.

"It doesn't really look like you. It's no good!" she says. "I've made you look like the Duke of Wellington!" But the portrait is very good—a bit idealized, perhaps, but excellent. I long to have it. "If you really want it, it's yours." And we move the easel indoors.

14.

"Why can't I sleep?" Bernstein asks. Again, it is hours past midnight. A cloudy night. The sea is restless. Small but insistent waves can be heard against the rocks below the villa. Sudden gusts of wind unsettle some of the outdoor furniture. It has not rained all summer. Perhaps tonight there will be rain. Lenny and I are in his studio. He is sitting at his desk.

"Last night, when I also couldn't sleep, I wrote this." He hands me a sheet of paper.

INSOMNIAD

Unable to sleep, we dream loud flowers
Anima blooming high-boom,
The loud flowers of the night.
We ingest our moon-protein
In our deepest yawns, nourished on lunacy.
We operate a passive factory!
Raw ergs come in, leave packaged, semi-cooked.
We prance half-blind on the tightrope,
I bouncing forward, I testing backward.
Together we make the loudest flowers ever
In our sleep-working factory
All alone. No one but me, and me.

"Is your insomnia a fear of nonexistence— perhaps of nonsignificance?" I ask. "Who knows!" Lenny answers. "I've been trying to find out for years what this nonsleep is all about. However, there are numerous nights when either I can't fall asleep, or fall asleep and then wake up in a state of wild alarm. Then I go padding to my studio and read or think, or sometimes turn on the radio, or compose (though that's hard to do, because in the middle of the night when you can't sleep, especially if you've taken a sleeping pill, you're pretty groggy).

"But very often, in those wee hours, I get a great deal done. Often I study. I find I can do that even with a sleeping pill. Composing is hard because that takes tremendous inner force. I find also that I can release ideas madly, that I get notions for a book, or an opera, for a show, and I make notes."

Bernstein searches for something on his desk. He finds a sheaf of notes clipped together. "Here's what I mean. Some of this is undecipherable, mainly because the writing in those hours can be very scribbly, and in many cases I find that I don't recognize the words. I can't remember having written down pages of this stuff." He hands it to me.

I look through the notes. My eye catches on one dated August 25, 1966, Bernstein's birthday of last year. The notes are legibly written, with very neat paragraphs. They describe a piece to be performed in a concert hall at the opening of a program. It is called *Prelude:*

" Full orchestra on stage: There is a chair between podium and the concertmaster. A guitar leans against it. At the other side of the podium a piano stands ready, lid open. Within the curve of the piano sits a well-dressed Negro. He has entered with the orchestra. Everything that happens is slow and quiet. L.B. in conventional tails enters conventionally without bowing. Sits in chair next to podium. Takes guitar and tunes it, carefully. L.B. says, while tuning, very slowly: "I love." The effect is ghastly. A long pause. Tittering in the house. The Negro says: "The audience thinks he's forgotten his lines. The audience thinks he's putting us on. The audience is curiously embarrassed." L.B. puts down guitar. Walks to piano and plays a ravishing new piece of about three minutes—romantic and intimate. L. B., from piano: "I love. *Amo, ergo sum.*" The audience thinks he is too pretentious! The audience thinks: "Perhaps this is some kind of ceremony." The audience is not unpleasantly bored. L.B. goes to podium. Conducts an improvisation of about three minutes. Returns to chair. The Negro says: "The audience thinks he ought to get up and walk out. The audience thinks, 'I am ashamed even to nudge my neighbor.'" The audience is piously angry. L.B. tunes guitar again, plays one chord. Sings: "I love." There is a lingering oboe phrase followed by a sad, falling viola figure. L.B. says: "I am going to die one day. So's this whole audience." A flute phrase, like a birdcall. L.B. says: "The audience thinks, 'Poor man, poor stuff.'" The audience thinks: "Why does he stoop to this East Village trash?" The audience is almost compassionate. L.B. goes to podium. Conducts one long pianissimo chord in which every member of the orchestra, including the percussion, chooses a note, any note, and holds it for a very long time, very softly. It is then gently cut off. The Negro now speaks: "The audience thinks, 'That must be the end.'" The audience thinks: "Thank the Lord!" The audience is deeply relieved. L.B. says: "Not yet. This must still be said. War is stupid. Men are stupid to make war. It is inexcusable that men still make war." The viola phrase again, during which L.B. exits. "

"It's no good," says Lenny. "It's a germ. Who is the Negro, I wonder? Sitting there, saying practically nothing?"

There is an elaborate outline about the Biblical characters David, Jonathan, and Saul, in terms of an operatic love triangle. "It's almost impossible to put on the stage. But there must be a way," Lenny says.

The challenge of doing the impossible has always fascinated Bernstein, the composer. After he had written *On the Town*, he had his heart set on writing an opera based on the Maxwell Anderson play *Winterset*. Some years later he became intrigued with James M. Cain's novel *Serenade*, which he and playwright Arthur Laurents thought would make a fascinating musical. But both these projects came to naught, although Bernstein and Laurents together with Jerome Robbins finally did collaborate on another seemingly impossible show, *West Side Story*. Prior to this, Bernstein and Lillian Hellman brought a musical version of Voltaire's *Candide* to the stage. It was a difficult, not entirely successful venture, but one which still has many ardent and loyal admirers, and one for which Lenny continues to feel great fondness. Another offbeat theater project, Thornton Wilder's *The Skin of Our Teeth* was to have brought together the original collaborators of *On the Town*. Bernstein, together with Robbins and Comden and Green, labored for six months during Lenny's sabbatical from the Philharmonic in 1965. For some reason, it didn't work out, and *Skin of Our Teeth* was abandoned.

Lenny's sense of challenge was to revive when he returned to New York from Italy. Jerome Robbins came to him with a short play by Berthold Brecht called *The Exception and the Rule*. He felt it could be turned into a pertinently satiric work if most of the characters were played by Negroes. A play about moral and economic exploitation set in the 1930's could be transformed, Robbins thought, into a contemporary musical drama of racial exploitation, done not turgidly but hilariously, with the leading character—a diabolical merchant—a sort of stand-up comic, in the manner of Phil Silvers or Zero Mostel, and the rest of the cast Negro.

Thus in New York in the winter of 1967-68, Bernstein was hard at work on the project, despite his grueling schedule with the Philharmonic. He and Robbins worked for weeks, late into the night, fashioning a book that would work, first with lyricist Jerry Leiber and then with Stephen Sondheim. At the time, Lenny told me, "I got excited about the project because it's *so* impossible, *so* problematic, and that is why, weeks and weeks later, we are still in the discussion stage."

However, to his own amazement, Bernstein wrote several numbers, and many bits and pieces of other sections. Still, he and his collaborators were continually trying to arrive at a clear approach. As Lenny put it, "What do we *really* mean? And which Negroes are we talking about? And who are we to write about Negroes, anyway? Is it *us* writing about Negroes doing Brecht? Or are *we* the Negroes who are doing it? Or is it *this* company of Negro actors? Or, maybe we should put it all in Africa. Make it *those* Negroes."

The sense of challenge. Leonard Bernstein thrives on it. I hand Lenny back his sheaf of insomniac notes. Outside the wind has subsided. There would be no rain after all.

15.

Time moves. It is August. In a few days Leonard Bernstein will celebrate his forty-ninth birthday. In a little more than a week, the Bernsteins will fly back to New York. Lenny will once more embark on a Philharmonic season which starts with a tour of Canada, including Expo 67 in Montreal. Later in the year, there will be many more commitments.

Lenny, sitting on the terrace, looks into a calm sea. Everything is so calm now and so quiet and so removed from what his life will be like in the year ahead. He shakes his head at the prospect and falls into a long silence. It is now late afternoon. For weeks I have tried to interest Lenny and Felicia in making a trip to Sardinia, some seven hours away by boat from Ansedonia. Lenny seems so "down" at the moment that I suggest the trip again. It would be an end-of-the-summer adventure for us all. We would take the car along, then drive across the island, visit the Emerald Coast, stay a day or two, then return home in time to celebrate his birthday.

To my surprise, Lenny perks up. "When should we leave?" he asks. "How about right this minute?" I answer. "Are you mad?" Then: "O.K., let's ask Felicia." Felicia is all for it. They decide the children should stay behind. Grown-ups only this time around. I dash to the phone and make a hotel reservation in Alghero, the city we decide to make our stopping point. I check on the boat leaving for Sardinia. It leaves in two hours, from Civitavecchia, which is nearly two hours away

New work in progress: Developing a Brechtian play with Jerry Leiber (center) and Jerome Robbins

from Ansedonia.

The villa now becomes the scene of a mad rush. The servants are in an uproar. Dinner was to be served in an hour. But Felicia decides we must eat sooner, if at all. The children become excited: "You'll never make the boat! There won't be time to eat! You'll get there too late!"

Somehow dinner is served. Everything, including a dessert that took hours to prepare, gets eaten in a tremendous, hilarious rush. The servants fly in and out of the kitchen bringing one dish after another. They are out of breath and not a little out of control. No meal was ever served this way. At the table, Lenny keeps saying, "This is madness!" I keep saying, "This is glorious!"

Felicia has dashed into the bedroom and thrown a few things in a small suitcase. There is no time for me to go back to my villa for a change of clothes. I must stay in the blue jeans and shirt I have on. (My wife is in Florence and obviously can't be of help in bringing anything over.) Lenny lends me a heavy sweater.

At last we sit in the car. Lenny drives like a house afire. It really does begin to look as though we might not make the boat. It has gotten dark. The road speeds by at a dizzying pace. The children had kept saying, "We'll see you back in four hours!" But Civitavecchia is suddenly very near. We finally arrive at the port. The boat is, indeed, about to leave. Have we time to purchase a ticket? (No reservations by phone were possible.) Yes, but we must hurry. The ticket office is across the square from the port. Lenny and I run and purchase tickets. Felicia is attending to the car, which must be hoisted by net onto the boat. Lenny and I get back to the boat just as the car is about to be lifted up. The crewmen are holding up the departure for this operation. Suddenly, by some quirky misunderstanding,

Lenny thinks he must sit in the car as it's being hoisted. He gets into the car and sits at the wheel. The men are about to give the sign. The net begins to lift. But they see Lenny sitting in the car. Angrily, the men give another sign to stop the hoisting. Lenny is not supposed to sit in the car while it's being hoisted into the air. The net is lowered again. Lenny gets out. Felicia screams with laughter. "Well, I thought I heard them say to get in the car!" says Lenny, abashed. "I thought so, too," says Felicia. "What a humiliation!" says Lenny, laughing. "Can you see George Szell doing this sort of thing?" We are the last to dash up the plank. We have made it! The boat leaves immediately.

An awful boat. Smelly and uncomfortable. Ghastly food. I begin to feel guilty for having suggested this trip. But Lenny and Felicia take everything in their stride and seem happy to be on the excursion. We have to spend the night in small, unattractive cabins. Suddenly exhaustion overcomes us all and we decide to retire. We shall land in Sardinia at 5 a.m.

Breakfast, consisting of lukewarm coffee and lukewarm eggs, frustratingly prepares us for our debarkation. The arid cliffs and mountains of Sardinia have come into view. In a few minutes we land. And now we sleepily walk off the boat, find our car, get in, and prepare for the four-hour journey across the island to Alghero and the Hotel Porto Conte.

Four hours! Time to talk, time to listen. Time to look at the incredible black and yellow landscape of Sardinia, a dry and awesome landscape, even a bit chilling. Lenny drives fast. This early the roads are empty of cars. He begins to feel exhilarated on the open road. The light is amazingly clear, a hot light, a stark, aggressive light. For the thousandth time that summer I think: Perhaps this is the moment to elicit the story of the debut. Lenny is captive in the car, there are hours of driving before us, no Mrs. Thorne to announce an arrival, no schedule. So I pop the question.

To my greatest surprise, Lenny turns to me and says quietly, "It all happened on November 14, 1943." I can't believe it. He is going to tell it—and without my usual prodding! Felicia offers a small yawn. (She had not closed an eye during the entire crossing.) "I may well take a long nap," she says, nestling into her seat. But only for a few minutes. The landscape is too beautiful, too intriguing for her to miss. And so, without interruption, Lenny embarks on the story of his fabulous New York Philharmonic debut and its incredible aftermath.

November 14—Aaron Copland's birthday. You see how it all worked out! The night before was Jennie Tourel's Town Hall debut at which she was singing my songs. I was terribly excited by that. I was going to have music of mine performed at Town Hall! I went to that, of course. My songs seemed to please, and I bowed. Oh, I can't tell you the excitement. I was on top of the world.

Jennie had a party afterwards at her apartment—which was full of all her many friends—and lots of drinking. I got to the piano, as was my wont in those days, and I sang blues and entertained (myself more than the others). I must have stayed there till three or four in the morning. It was very late, I drank a lot and celebrated. Then I went home, went to sleep, and was awakened out of an enormous hangover by the telephone ringing at 9 a.m. There was Bruno Zirato saying, "You're going to have to conduct the concert at three this afternoon because Bruno Walter [the guest conductor that week] cannot make it. He's ill."

Rodzinski was at his farm in Stockbridge, resting. Here it was Sunday. In those days the Sunday afternoon concert was broadcast nationwide, and every conductor considered it the most important concert of the week.

It seemed just incredible to me that Bruno Walter should get sick and that this occasion should ever arise at all, because it had been fifteen years or more since any conductor had been sick at the Philharmonic. Why now? As it turned out, every conductor that season got sick. It got to the point where rumors were circulated that I was poisoning coffee. Or that my father had paid a certain enormous sum to get Bruno Walter to feign sickness, so that I could conduct. Unbelievable!

So there I was, nine o'clock in the morning, hung over, six hours away from this dreamlike debut. No chance of rehearsal! I did know the program well. It was a difficult program, but I had studied it particularly hard because it contained Strauss' *Don Quixote,* which I'd fallen in love with and which I really studied late every night at the piano, and from a miniature score that I remember you had to turn on its side when the scoring got too big and had to be printed on two pages. I had also reread the apposite portions of Cervantes' novel, so that I was really deeply involved with the piece and its literary meaning. I was delighted with it.

Also on the program was the prelude to *Meistersinger* by Wagner, the overture to *Manfred* by Schumann (a fine piece that I hadn't known before), and a new piece by Miklos Rozsa called *Theme and Variations,* which is a very good piece of no particular consequence. I sort of knew all those pieces—and I sort of was ready. But no one can be ready for such a moment, especially without rehearsal—and with a hangover. I remember Zirato saying that Bruno Walter had offered to go over the scores with me, which I thought was very sweet of him. I got dressed and ran to his hotel where he gave me his scores, and showed me where he cut off, where he didn't cut off, where he waited a beat before going on to the next variation, or whatever. He couldn't have been sweeter. There he was, all wrapped up in blankets and very ill, indeed. But he went through all this with me, very patiently. What a kind and wonderful man! He gave me his blessings and I went back to Carnegie Hall.

I went into the Carnegie Hall drugstore, which was then at the corner, where a coffee shop now is. The pharmacist there was a friend; I told him about my having to conduct that afternoon (he was the first to know) and how nervous I was about it. He said, "Look, take these two little pills and put them in your pocket, and before you go on, take them. They'll steady you." I had never taken pills. One was phenobarbital, to quiet the nerves. The other was something to do the opposite. So I put these two little pills in my pocket.

The other people I let know were my parents, who happened to be in New York that weekend for the great event of Jennie Tourel's recital which, until then, was the high point of my life. Zirato had let Rodzinski know about Walter's illness and had gone through the formalities of asking him to come down from Stockbridge to conduct, but, of course, that was out of the question. First of all, he wasn't up on the program. And, after all, it was my job. That's what an assistant conductor was for. They also alerted Koussevitzky, who sent me a telegram which I got during intermission saying, "Listening now. Wonderful!"

By the way, Rodzinski had heard me conduct at Tanglewood. I think that convinced him to hire me. And I think Koussy had talked to him about me. (I'm looking for some real explanation, besides God.)

So here I was. Of course, my emotions were all over the place. I didn't know what was going to happen. I had never conducted a full program. Even at Tanglewood, it was always a piece you conducted. But here I was conducting coast-to-coast, on the radio, this full program. The Philharmonic alerted *The New York Times* and Olin Downes came.

Well, it's legendary now, that debut. The audience was out of its head. I remember the pain, at the beginning, of Bruno Zirato going on stage to make the announcement about the change of conductors. The groan that went up from the audience! After all, this utterly unknown conductor coming on. I remember standing there and trembling and feeling already rejected by this audience. I took those two pills from my pocket and flung them across the floor. I said to myself, "No sir! I'm going to do this on my own!" The groan—it was like hearing the bull roar in the pen! And the torero decides at that moment that he is going to have his day.

Out I strode in my funny double-breasted suit. (I couldn't wear the tails for an afternoon concert.) There was a light patter of applause, and I went wildly into the three crazy opening chords of *Manfred*. It was like a great electric shock. From then on, I was just sailing. I don't know what happened. But those three chords I will never forget! *Zum-zai-zam!* Pause. In that pause, I knew that everything was going to be all right. Ah, those three chords were so glorious! The orchestra was really with me, giving me everything they had, all their attention. It was really a pretty beautiful concert. I don't remember it, but I know this from air-tapes of the broadcast which I listened to later.

It was a great day. Rodzinski also sent a telegram saying how exciting it all was over the radio. And backstage! Everybody pressed in around me. Immediately afterward there were crowds—and my parents streaming tears—and friends who had heard about it. I went out to dinner with my mother and father. I got quite tipsy, I remember. We had a big celebration at dinner. The next morning the *Times* had the story on the front page!

Now, Rodzinski returns from Stockbridge. He was so proud of me! "You see," he said, "God was right and I was right, but now you mustn't let this go to your head. Now, more than ever, you must kneel and give yourself to God." And I said, "Yes, of course." But, of course, I was swimming in the delirious bliss of success, because there was not a moment when there wasn't some magazine or newspaper at my door. Interviews with *The New Yorker,* and *Harper's Bazaar,* and *Vogue*—and, well, name it.

Shortly after my debut, Arthur Judson had called me into his office and said, "I have it all planned out. You will have the Philharmonic before you're thirty. It will take three years. I have it all arranged. You'll go to Los Angeles next year. You'll cut your teeth. You'll make your repertoire. Then I'll move you to Cleveland for two years. Then you'll be ready for the Philharmonic."

I said, "I'm not interested." He was enraged. He just couldn't get over it. I tried to explain to him that I wanted to compose, that I wanted to be free to see the world. I didn't want to be tied down to one orchestra in one city. He had never been refused such a thing before. I mean, to refuse the New York Philharmonic! Which he was offering to a boy of twenty-five. We never had much of a relationship after that.

The aftermath was very exciting. But the more excited I got about it, the more Rodzinski would say, "But now, more than ever...." And he began to change his attitude toward me. I still went on with my work. I didn't abandon rehearsals. I wasn't suddenly running around as the toast of New York. I mean, I had this wonderful thing, but I also had my job,

which I kept doing faithfully, although a great deal of time was going to interviews. Gradually, Rodzinski became less friendly.

The next month, I think, the guest conductor was Howard Barlow, and he got sick. He couldn't conduct the Thursday concert. In fact, he gave up Thursday, so that he would be well enough to conduct the Sunday broadcast concert. So, I did that concert also, but with a rehearsal because there was time for preparation. That program consisted of the Beethoven Violin Concerto, with Albert Spalding as soloist, and Delius' *Paris.* It began with the Brahms *Haydn Variations.* I had one rehearsal, and that again went very excitingly.

This time Virgil Thomson, who was then critic of the *Herald Tribune,* wrote one of those unbelievable reviews. It was the Second Coming of You-know-who. He guessed that the secret of my conducting was my incredible rhythmic sense. Something like that. Rhythmic understanding or rhythmic insight—I don't remember exactly—which I possessed "to a far greater degree than any contemporary conductor with the possible exception of Thomas Beecham." That I remember word for word. An incredible sentence.

By this time, Rodzinski's patience was wearing a little thin, because as far as he was concerned this was his first season at the New York Philharmonic and the whole excitement seemed to be about me. I mean, any paper, any magazine he picked up that talked about the Philharmonic was about me, while he wasn't getting any comparable publicity.

He read the *Tribune* review with some rancor and immediately began to play the works of Virgil Thomson to rectify the situation. It was shortly thereafter, as a matter of fact, that he walked into Arthur Judson's office and wrecked the furniture. Turned over the file cabinets, went absolutely out of his mind, and

107

screamed at Judson, "What are you doing to me! This is a conspiracy. You are all conspiring against me." (This was his big problem. He had a dreadful sense of persecution.) "You are giving Bernstein all the publicity and me none."

Judson and Zirato said, "Now, look, this is ridiculous. Nobody is conspiring against you. It just happens that this is an attractive story and everybody likes it, and they want to print it. But it's nothing against you and you're still the conductor." But Rodzinski wouldn't take any of it. He made a terrible scene and they had to start a very special publicity campaign for him. Suddenly all the papers came out with pictures of Rodzinski in his bee-mask. Rodzinski milking his cow, etc. But, somehow, it didn't make any difference.

Meanwhile, the preceding autumn, Fritz Reiner had sent me a letter from Pittsburgh saying, "I have just been looking at your *Jeremiah* symphony and I like it very much." He asked me to come and conduct it, and do another piece, the *Firebird*—half a program. This was to be in January. I had already arranged for it, and it was put in my contract with Zirato that I had to be away one week in Pittsburgh.

So, the time was now approaching. At this very vulnerable moment, Rodzinski began to go around sniffing, brandishing large handkerchiefs, and saying, "I think I've got a fever." I do believe he had a cold, but I think it was a classic psychosomatic case.

The day I had to leave for Pittsburgh I went in to say good-bye. There he stood, sneezing and coughing. He looked at me with accusing. rheumy eyes and said, "Just when I need you!" I said, "Oh, please! This is the biggest moment of my life. I'm going to conduct my symphony for the first time—a world premiere! Please don't make me feel badly about it." "No, no!" he said. "Don't think of me, please. I'll be all

right." You know, real Jewish mother tactics.

I went. My father and my sister went with me (the symphony is dedicated to my father). Again it was wild! Front pages, banner headlines, a shouting audience. Jennie had to be the soloist, of course. She was, by now, my dear friend and collaborator. She sang marvelously and the orchestra played wonderfully. It was so moving, and Reiner was so excited. And the *Firebird!* I was just on fire!

Meanwhile, back in New York things had gone very badly. Rodzinski had, indeed, collapsed with flu and they had gotten William Steinberg, who was later to become the director of the Pittsburgh Symphony. You see how these things go round-robin!

Rodzinski had apparently prayed, "lost his ego," and he did welcome me back. "Hy'a, kid," and a big embrace. Then, just like that, he turned very cold. He would ignore me, be very brusque. Then again, he'd suddenly be full of love and light. It wasn't very pleasant. And yet I was sailing.

Meanwhile, back in October sometime, there came a knock at my door one night, and in walked a fellow called Jerome Robbins. He said, "I've been sitting in Central Park with Oliver Smith (whom I knew) and he told me to come and see you."

Jerry was then a dancer in the Ballet Theater, one of three whom Lucia Chase had offered a chance to choreograph an original ballet. She gave them money and rehearsal time. It was Jerry's first ballet and he had asked Oliver Smith to be the scenic designer of his ballet. He had some notion about three sailors on shore leave, and girls, and fun.

He had also been in touch with that same Miklos Rozsa, whose *Theme and Variations* I had done at my Philharmonic debut, to write the music. Rozsa had already written a piece called *First Sailor's Dance*, which I still have

Text continues on page 130

Koussevitzky cuff links, Mitropoulos cross

Family congratulations backstage

Continued from page 108

somewhere, a piano piece, which is real rustic, Hungarian stuff. It had nothing to do with what Jerry had in mind, however, and he was in despair. So when Jerry consulted with Oliver Smith about doing the scenery, he happened to ask if Oliver knew an American composer who could do the music. Oliver mentioned me and said, "He's living in Carnegie Hall. Why don't you go and see him?" Which Jerry did, and that accounts for the knock at the door in the middle of the night.

He talked to me about this ballet. I thought it was an exciting idea. I played him some stuff at the piano that I had just thought up and was fooling around with, which became the opening tune of *Fancy Free*. I had that tune and it seemed exactly suited to his ballet. He went wild. "That's it! That's it!" he screamed, and we were off.

I began to write *Fancy Free* whenever I could, between rehearsals and appearances and interviews and Pittsburgh and everything. *Fancy Free* was to have its premiere in April—it now being 1944. I told Rodzinski that I was writing a ballet, but I didn't realize that he would use even this for a final accusation—that I wasn't doing my job. "When he's writing a ballet, how could he possibly be studying his scores"—that sort of thing. But so far I had not been lacking. When I had to know the scores, I knew them. Indeed, I knew all the scores. I studied very hard. I worked very hard. And I also composed.

Then came the terrible day—in March, I believe. Oh, I forgot to say that shortly after my Pittsburgh success, I received a telegram from Koussevitzky saying, "I've heard about the success of *Jeremiah* in Pittsburgh. Would you come and conduct it in Boston?" I asked permission to have that week in Boston, and Rodzinski said, "Oh, of course! I can't keep you from the Boston Symphony." But, again,

with a lot of "Don't think of me" thrown in. I went to Boston. It was again a big smash. It was so exciting because it was my father's city, and my city, and it meant a great deal to me. While I was there, I had a telegram from Rodzinski, whom I'd last seen in high dudgeon, saying, "Congratulations on your great success in Boston. Will you conduct a whole program with the Philharmonic? Any works of your choice, but including *Jeremiah*." Well, I can't tell you what a surprise this was. Playing my own piece with the orchestra I was closest to. I was finally going to do a full program of my own devising, fully rehearsed, and including my own symphony!

I came back to New York in a state of excitement, and flung myself into Rodzinski's arms and said, "Aren't you wonderful and generous!" and words like that. Well, everything was warmth and light for about a day or two, and then it started again. Anything would start him off. Seeing my picture in the paper. A chance remark. People, thinking he would feel good, would congratulate him on his assistant. Of course, it was the last thing he wanted to hear. He couldn't stand my name anymore.

The concert came about. I remember playing the Italian Symphony by Mendelssohn, Aaron's *El Salón México*, my symphony—and I can't remember what else. The three performances were very exciting. Standing ovations, stuff like that. But a terrible review by Virgil of my symphony. He said, "As brilliant as he is as an executor, so dreadful is he as a composer"—something like that. He called it imitative, derivative nonsense, things like that. He hated it. I remember he wrote, "He writes his brasses high!" and conceded that the orchestration was thrilling. Anyhow, the concert went marvelously, and Rodzinski went into the dumps.

One day I fell sick at a morning rehearsal.

I had a stomach ache, or something. I told the personnel manager that I was ill and that I would be upstairs in my room if I was needed, that I had to go up and lie down, which I did. In the afternoon I felt better. I went out to get a haircut at the Essex House barber shop. And there in the next chair sat Rodzinski. He glowered at me and said, "I thought you were sick!" I said, "I was, and I feel better now." That was it. We sat in silence having our hair cut for half an hour.

Promptly the next morning, at 9:30, before his rehearsal, he went to Judson's office and said, "Now! Now I have him! There's your famous Bernstein! Caught in the act. He said he was sick, and there he was in the barber shop." Somebody also had seen me walking my dog. It was true; I had taken my dog out. Judson called me up. "What's all this about you and Rodzinski and the barber shop? What's going on?" I said, "I have no idea. I was feeling ill during the morning rehearsal. I left to go upstairs to lie down. By afternoon I felt better, took my dog out for a walk, brought him back, and went and got a haircut. What have I done?"

Judson said, "I don't know, but whatever it is, we can't have this at the Philharmonic. There's an atmosphere of murder! You've got to go backstage before this morning's rehearsal and apologize to him, because he's on the warpath." I said, "Apologize for what?" He said, "I don't know, but whatever it is, just apologize! Make things well again."

I went backstage to Rodzinski's dressing room—and before I could say, "Good morn...." —I didn't get "good morning" out—he grabbed me by the throat and pinned me to the wall. He was brutally strong. He had this huge, almost humped back, like a bull, solid muscle. And he was calling me a liar, a cheat—I don't know what. I squirmed free somehow, or somebody came into the room and he had to let go, because he was killing me.

That poor man. When I think of the suffering he must have gone through to bring him to such a point! It's heartbreaking when you think about it. But at that moment I wasn't heartbroken. I was angry and scared. I ran into Judson's office, panting, with these black and blue marks on my throat, and said, "I've just gone in to apologize, as I was told to, and I got this curious greeting. What do I do now?" Judson said, "I think you better stay away from him for a while. Don't go to rehearsals. I'll arrange something. I'll tell him something."

So I stayed away for a week or so, and I worked very hard on *Fancy Free,* because that was coming up in a couple of weeks. I got it finished and orchestrated. We got it on and it was a glorious success. There were thirty-odd minutes of screaming at the Metropolitan Opera House. I conducted it myself. It was terribly exciting. Sol Hurok came and he said we must do it everywhere, on tour, San Francisco, the Hollywood Bowl, and I must conduct it. He also made me a managerial offer for life. I remember he took me to lunch at the Russian Tea Room and said, "Look, you'll have all these concerts, but I can give you much more than that. I can give you security. How much do you need to live on a year? What do you need?" I thought at the most I needed $15,000 to live well. I was thinking in terms of living at Carnegie Hall, with no dependents, and eating at the Russian Tea Room. That was life. So he said, "All right. I'll tell you what. I'll guarantee you $15,000 a year, come hell or high water, and you'll do all the concerts that I arrange for you, and whatever is over the $15,000, of course, I keep." I never had any head for business, but something rang bells that told me that this was some form of slavery. I turned him down. He never really forgave me for that, or for not saying, "How about making it $100,000?" Yet I am very fond of Sol Hurok and admire him greatly.

Can you imagine the sort of year I had? Everything beginning on my birthday. Can you imagine? Following the lean and hungry years, suddenly—beginning with that day—everything that could happen happened. Everything you could dream about.

With the premiere of *Fancy Free*, everybody at the Philharmonic realized that I couldn't possibly continue. For many reasons, but mainly because Rodzinski couldn't tolerate it. I didn't see Rodzinski for a long time after his attempt to strangle me. Judson had told me to stay away. Much later I saw him again. I went to his concerts. We said, "Hello." But it was just that. I mean, he didn't invite me to his house and no mention was ever made of the incident. I saw him last here in Italy where, as you know, he died of a heart attack. **"**

That was it. Leonard Bernstein had relived the most unbelievable year of his life. The hours had flown by; the sign ahead of us read Alghero.

Sardinia was a good idea. Bernstein felt as relaxed and happy as he had been all summer. He and Felicia swam, took long walks, explored ancient villages, visited churches and ruins. While in Alghero, they met film director Joseph Losey, who was shooting *Boom*, a film based on Tennessee Williams' play, *The Milk Train Doesn't Stop Here Anymore*.

The trip back to Ansedonia, mountainous and beautiful, is taken at high speed. Lenny drives very fast, yet is always in command of the car. Behind the wheel he is possessed by the pleasure of speed.

At the midway point we stop at a railroad crossing. Felicia has noticed that the road is flanked by masses of raspberry briers. She makes us get out of the car so that we might pick some. The landscape extending before us seems suspended in time. A vast cascading panorama of sun-drenched valleys falls away from us—magically, atavistically. The air is pure and light. We move from the road into this landscape. Lenny leads us through a narrow arbor into the valley. There are many more raspberries to be picked here. In a moment, we stand in the open fields. In the distance, the sound of sheep bells is heard. It is a melancholy, sweetly dissonant sound. We stand listening, almost transfixed by the scene before us, the bells intensifying the vastness and tranquility around us. Lenny closes his eyes and breathes deeply, savoring these moments of complete peace. We walk back to the car. Standing near the railroad crossing is the gatekeeper, a small, intensely blue-eyed, middle-aged Sardinian. He seems happy to see people in this uninhabited spot. Lenny engages him in conversation. The gatekeeper speaks of the loneliness of his job, of how he'd much prefer to be a shepherd, as he had been for most of his life. He speaks of his family living in a small house some miles away. He invites us to come home with him—to have some wine and to meet his little daughter who can play the guitar. The man removes his cap, revealing a head of pitch-black curls. "My little girl's hair is exactly like mine," he tells us, smiling. But time is running short. Lenny and Felicia want to get back to the children. We decline the gatekeeper's kind invitation. He stands waving a long time as we drive away.

The boat trip to the mainland is dreary. At last we reach Civitavecchia. In two more hours we shall be home. Felicia makes a phone call in advance. The children, the servants, and my wife, child, and dog are all waiting at the Bernstein villa. Our reception is full of squeals, hugs, and kisses.

16.

Jamie has decided that Lenny's birthday party, on the following evening, should include a series of children's games—musical chairs, spin-the-bottle, post office. She and I have a conference about it. Alexander joins us. In a moment, Nina and my daughter Julia are in on the conference. We are sitting by the pool. But Nina and Julia quickly tire of our talk, and they jump in—swimming, laughing, and having a little chat all their own. I catch bits and snatches of it: "Do you like the stars in the sky, Nina?" asks Julia. "Oh, yes," she replies, "they're very pretty and very stylish and very gobbled inside!" "What kind of moon do you like?" Julia asks. "I like the kind of moon that's new," says Nina. "Because the moon that is new comes to shine around the world, you see. And the stars between the moon become silver and gold in little points."

Nina and Julia were constant playmates in Ansedonia. Despite the difference of their ages —Nina was five and Julia eight—they managed to find endless amusement in each other's company. They invented games out of other games, spent hours snorkeling and sloshing in the pool, spent hours at the piano, did a lot of drawing together, played card games, sang, danced, and cavorted like otters in the sun. What was remarkable was the complete ease with which the relationship endured the entire summer. The girls spontaneously created their own world. This was, to a great extent, Nina's doing.

In the Bernstein household, Nina has found a role for herself. She wants everybody to laugh, to be entertained, to be happy. She has an instinctive nose for the climate of a room. She has absolute pitch when it comes to sensing moods, and when the moods are happy she has a way of intensifying and projecting herself into them, so that the elation becomes even stronger.

The Bernstein children are a trio of indi-
viduals. They do not seem to overlap in character or resemblance. There is no Bernstein mold. Whatever the problems of having a world-famous father with an uncontrollably dominant personality, the children stand as very separate entities. Because of the sense of their own individuality, they can, in fact, stand their ground with considerable effectiveness in the face of the phenomenon of Leonard Bernstein. In a way, Lenny tries to elicit from them this effective competition and friendly rivalry. The standards, however, are very high.

First came Jamie, born September 8, 1952. Then came Alexander Serge (for Koussevitzky), on July 7, 1955. Last came Nina, born February 28, 1962. When the children are with their parents, they instinctively know what is expected of them; when they are by themselves they behave more like children, working out their own scraps and scrapes. With their mother and father, they are almost industriously well-behaved. Felicia Bernstein believes in instilling a strong sense of individual responsibility in her children, both personal and social. They are, after all, Leonard Bernstein's children. But more importantly, she believes that life will be easier for them if they follow and observe amenities, not as mechanical proprieties but as a personal point of departure that will always be second nature to them in later life. Thus, she insists on their being well-groomed, on their rising when a grown-up walks into the room, on shaking hands in a direct, friendly manner, on being responsive to adult questions and conversation addressed to them; and at the same time on recognizing that they are children who must not take the floor or overstay their time. This arrangement is based on fairness and an acknowledged acceptance of everyone's role in the family. In short, when there are guests the Bernstein children are around briefly and pleasantly, and then return to their

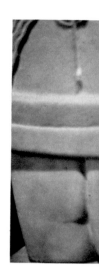

135

own work, play, or friends. This acceptance of roles stems from a very close familial life.

The closeness is doubly based: on Felicia's Latin descent and specifically Chilean upbringing, and on Lenny's Hasidic heritage. The combination of these two strong traditions creates an atmosphere of an almost defensive privacy and warmth, an atmosphere conducive to the flowering of individual personality. At its best, it makes for a multileveled rapport between members of the family. It can range from an exuberant, rambunctious verbal punning in which Jamie and Alexander try to outdo their father—often successfully— to a genuine absorption in and concern with each other's feelings, ideas, and thoughts. Lenny and Felicia consistently encourage the children to be as articulate as possible about their feelings and confusions.

Lenny is the inciter of learning, the gamester, the instigator of energetic activity. Felicia is the one who must insist on the regimen —table manners, bedtime, homework, piano practice, neatness. She also guides and supervises the children's social life. (The Bernsteins' Spanish-speaking nurse, Julia, has been aiding Felicia in these tasks since Jamie was a tot. All the children, incidentally, speak Spanish fluently.)

If Lenny is a source of stimulation—even overstimulation—Felicia is there to ameliorate the effusiveness by good-naturedly bringing everyone down to earth. In the Bernstein family, Felicia is the great stabilizer. Given the overwhelming energy and presence of their father, Jamie, Alexander, and Nina reflect an assurance and self-confidence that marks them as happy children. They know they are loved and they love in return.

At fifteen, Jamie has the maturity and intelligence of a girl older than her years. She has an uncanny command of words, stemming, of course, from Lenny's own articulateness, his love of word games and puzzles, a love she shares with him. Jamie shows talent, as might be expected, as a writer of poetry and prose. There is a great softness about Jamie; her features have the delicacy of a cameo. The eyes are a clear blue-gray, discerning and always thoughtfully observant. Somehow she seems happiest in the company of adults and has instinctive responses to their characters. Like all the Bernsteins, Jamie is extremely musical. Her pleasure is to sing, even more than to play the piano, and her voice is a touching alto. She is a voracious reader and, when put to the test, a splendid conversationalist. As the teen-ager of the family, she seems wise to the world. She views it with humor, impatience, often with consternation. But there is awareness and wisdom in Jamie. She's not easily fooled.

The words "poignant" and "tender" apply perfectly to Alexander. At twelve, he is perhaps the most sensitive member of the family. He feels the burden of his maleness; it comes in the form of challenge as much from his mother and sisters as from his father. The opposing, often contradictory forces by which he is surrounded have tended to make him vulnerable to his own feelings. They frequently brim over and spill, leaving him perplexed, enraged, sometimes painfully confused. But his maleness is secure. His passion for sports of any kind has made him his father's frequent companion on skiing trips to Colorado and sailing trips in Italy. He is a superb swimmer and water-skier, and an excellent tennis player. What is more, he can be fanatically competitive. There is no physical activity that does not engage him completely. At times his sense of competition is so strong that losing a game may send him off in tears of rage.

Alexander is a small, handsome child. He has his father's energy, his father's tremendous curiosity. He is full of questions and full of ideas. His adoration of Lenny is all-consuming. The summer in Ansedonia made clear this adoration, as father and son were practically inseparable. The Hebrew lessons, the long, indefatigable swims, the walks, the talks gave Alexander a measure of his own identity.

Sitting here, at this poolside, I look at Leonard Bernstein's children. They are engaging young people—intelligent, aware, and interesting. Nina, Julia, and Alexander decide to play a game of cards. They move to the terrace. Jamie and I remain by the pool. I ask her what it's like being Leonard Bernstein's daughter. Being an articulate girl, she talks at length about it:

"I've always known that Daddy was famous. I've always been conscious of that fact. When I was in second grade I had a friend who used to call me "famous-father girl." I remember calling her "famous monkey-face" in return.

When I was smaller, I was embarrassed that he was my father. I wouldn't want anybody to know about it. And if they talked about it, I'd sort of...oh, I don't know.

I went to concerts then, but I was extremely bored by them and I didn't understand much. I'd go backstage and Daddy would say, "Well, did you understand anything?" and I'd say, "No."

But when I got older, I began to get much more conscious of Daddy—and so did my school friends. In fifth grade I really became more conscious, but it wasn't until much later that being Leonard Bernstein's daughter affected other people's behavior toward me. Some were a little scared of me, or awed, and some just didn't talk to me. I don't think it bothers my close friends. But do you remember the time Daddy kissed Mrs. Kennedy on television at the opening of Lincoln Center? Well, the turmoil at school the next day. It was absolutely hysterical. "Your father kissed Jacqueline Kennedy!" That was a big thing!

When I was smaller, Daddy was just Daddy. He was such a Daddy-Daddy! When I was small, Daddy was the Almighty, the utmost! I mean, nothing could be wrong! Of course, when I got older I realized that this was not the case. It came as a shock, with a bang, to discover that Daddy had faults.

What I like most about Daddy is that he's very human. He's about the most human being I've known. He's also very stubborn, extremely stubborn. As you know, even though he has a bad back he'll go ahead and do what's not good for him. He's very truthful. I don't think he knows how to lie. In fact, he may be a little too truthful for his own good. He's so outspoken.

He's a perennial teacher—perennial! If you're reading a book and ask him what "existentialism" means (I've never asked him that, by the way. I know better!), you get a lecture for the rest of the day. He'll give you the root of the word, plus a whole lecture on Greek, or God knows what—and, yes, he's *always* teaching. You hear it and you do absorb it. But he's always teaching, even when he doesn't know what he's talking about.

He's always teaching when he does the Young Peoples Concerts. I sometimes look over his shoulder when he writes the scripts, and sometimes I say, "No, you're not going to say that," because every now and then he says some things that aren't right, or uses words that aren't right. I did help him when he worked on that rock-and-roll special for television. I gave him all my records to work with. He'd ask me, "Where can I find an example of a bass line, or an example of hiked-up guitar sounds?" And I'd say, "I Saw Her Standing There," or

this one or that one. And I advised him.

Then he wrote his whole script out, and he said, "Look it over and see if I've made any mistakes." I looked it over and, of course, he hadn't made any mistakes, but I did question a lot of his language. He used words like "lingo," which I hate. So I changed the wording; that's all I did. (P.S. He wound up saying "lingo.")

Daddy helps me a lot, too. Especially when I do term papers for school. Also on imaginative work we have to do, to write. I read these things to him. Oh, the many lines he's changed for me! We had to write a sonnet this year, and I wrote it. He saw it and he changed a couple of lines. I left them in. They were much better than mine.

He helps me with math. They started teaching New Math just when I was learning Old Math. Daddy, who never studied New Math, comes and tells me what to do, but I say, "Daddy, that's *not* what we're supposed to do," and he says, "Yes, it is! Because...." And he finds a whole different way of going about it. Of course, I get even more confused, especially since I'm not very good at math.

As far as any personal problems are concerned, it depends on what the problem is whether I go to Mummy or to Daddy. There are certain problems I wouldn't dream of going to Daddy with, and, of course, vice versa. Problems about boys—and social problems—generally go to Mummy. Problems about school generally go to Daddy. But most of the problems never go to either of them.

Our family is very united. We are so outspoken with each other. The atmosphere is very free and easy. We sit five at the table and the atmosphere is very relaxed. It couldn't be better. In other words, the Daddy up there on the podium and the Daddy at home are two different people.

Of course, there are things wrong with Daddy. I mean, he does tend to overdo it with the teaching, and he does see things his way. What I mean is, even though he may be wrong and you can explain to him why he may be wrong, somehow, you can't swerve him. Once he gets an idea in his head, that's sort of it.

He's a very nonviolent man. He sometimes will get a little carried away and give us a little slap, but he doesn't really mean it. The trouble is he has such enormous hands, and they're so strong. I know he just pretends. I do remember being spanked twice, and they were very traumatic experiences for the very reason that they were so rare.

Then there are the interruptions. The business of interrupting Daddy. The whole Bernstein family has this thing about interrupting, because speech is such an important factor of our being together. Everyone has to have his say, and everyone has to put in his two bits exactly when he thinks of it. Everyone talks at once. Finally, Daddy says, "Stop it! Stop interrupting. Now I'm going to talk." And he talks. He also has a habit of swerving the conversation toward himself. I'm sure it's perfectly unconscious.

But Daddy is so generous. So kind. For birthdays we get enormous presents. Things are very different when he goes away on tour—especially if Mummy goes with him. There's such a paleness about the house. When we come home from school when Mummy is here, we always have tea. But when they're gone there seems to be a great tension, and a great gap, and a lack of warmth.

I can see myself following in Daddy's footsteps. At least as far as character traits are concerned. I know I have the same traits he has, especially some of his bad traits. I see them in me, and I know there is nothing I can do about them. For example, I interrupt a lot and find myself directing the conversation to myself. Horrible!

About boys? Well, I'm at an age when the boys haven't really matured more than the girls yet. I have not found anyone, but not anyone, not even idols in the movies, who have lived up to what I expect. I'm very worried. Intelligence is very important to me. I can see a handsome boy, but when I discover he's not intelligent—well, forget it. I suppose it's because Daddy is such a spectacular person in that department.

Anyway, to me the idea of being a housewife is the most boring thing I can think of. Although I adore music, I think I'd better not do anything involved with music. Despite the fact that it's easier to be the daughter of a famous man than to be a son.

I do think about Alexander. Sometimes I worry about him. First of all, he seems to have a big chip on his shoulder, perhaps about his father being such a great person. When Alexander grows up he wants to be a teacher. I think that would be very good. At one point, he said he wanted to be a psychiatrist, but I think he's dropped that idea. I think he should be a teacher. He's an excellent teacher—just the way he teaches Nina how to do things! I'd love to teach, myself, because if I write, which I would love to do, I can't *just* write. And I love people. People are what really interest me. At the moment I watch them more than being with them. I observe them. I love watching their characters.

As to my relationship with Alexander, it's about normal. I can still beat him up. That's the one thing that's not so normal. But somehow, since he was always sickly when he was small, and since Julia our nurse was always there, and since he was always such a shrimp—well, it sort of affected me. When Alexander was small, he was always sick. He's so hefty and fat now you wouldn't believe it.

He has this thing—he cries very easily. You may have noticed. For example, sometimes when he plays tennis and he loses it's as if—I can't explain it—it's just awful. He just dies. Sometimes he even hurls his racket on the court and he dashes off and runs to his room and probably has a good cry. But that phase seems to be passing. He's growing up.

Nina? This kid has really got it made! She's hysterical. She obviously has such a character! I think she's more stubborn than Daddy, which is pretty stubborn. She will have her own way when she grows up. She has a great sense of humor. She'll catch a good man there!

And Mummy! Mummy manages, period. She really manages. She is, I find, in a tremendously difficult position. She has to be a hostess. She has to be a personality. She has to be funny, and a good wife, and everything for Daddy, but without being more than Daddy. After all, she is also an artist. She has to keep back a little bit. Some of the time she is unhappy. Maybe she doesn't want to go out and meet a lot of people. Maybe she'd rather sit at home and paint or read. I sympathize with that feeling, because I know that feeling. But she goes and she does it, and she's a good sport.

I admire her so much. But I know I'm not going to be like Mummy. I wish I could be. I'm going to be much more like Daddy. I'm more like him. I'm more outgoing. I like doing crazy things. I would love to be like Mummy.

She protects me from a lot of things. She's very strong on manners. Ever since we were kids we were taught manners. Alexander has a little harder time with that than I have, because he's in the moon half the time, in a world of his own. The memories of my childhood are always going to be of Mummy telling me what to do in Spanish—*levántase! la mano!*

gracias!—whispered for years.

Mummy and Daddy. Sometimes I look at them and I say to myself, "Why the hell did they get married?" They are the two most opposite, most uncombining people. I just don't understand it. And yet it works. Besides, Daddy has grown up so in the last few years. Really, he's changed quite a lot. And I've changed immensely in the last few years.

Last year was my big turning point. Last year I really became what I'm obviously going to be when I grow up. I remember seeing it happen. There were two weeks there when I was home alone with Mummy (Daddy was away and Alexander was at camp). We were always with each other and Nina. And I remember sitting in Fairfield in a hammock, looking up in the trees, and I read a book, or swam, or played tennis, and somehow I suddenly found myself. I would sit down and just contemplate on things, and I think I uncovered and discovered what I really am. I haven't, of course, been thrust into life. I know it.

I do know it's better being Leonard Bernstein's daughter than being Leonard Bernstein's son. Alexander is, I suppose, expected to follow in his father's footsteps. Not so of a girl. She can always be a wife, although that's a pretty Victorian idea.

I find I'm very glad to be growing up in this particular period, in this time. When I was smaller I was always looking at things—at life —from somewhere else. I was always in the middle, looking down at the smaller ones, looking up at the larger ones. Always looking, always looking. Never being in it, never being a part of it.

Except for the time, I guess, when I was in sixth grade. That was when the Beatles came out. I was a Beatlemaniac. You're lucky you never saw me when I was a Beatlemaniac! I screamed when you said the word Beatles. But I had *such* a good time. I never had such a good time in my life as I had when I was in sixth grade. It was a very easy year. I had marvelous teachers. I had nothing in the world to care about. I had a marvelous time, and the Beatles came out! I was in love with all four of them. I bought their records and I knew them by heart. Thank God Daddy liked them too. Somehow they made me grow up faster. One time I met them—backstage when they were taping an Ed Sullivan Show. I cannot tell you the feelings! To be knocking at a door and to know that behind that door were the Beatles! And the feeling of knocking at that door... well, it was indescribable. They inspired me a lot. I wrote endless, countless poems. And the junk I collected! I have one suitcase, one scrapbook, and one gigantic manila folder packed with just Beatle propaganda and junk and stuff. And the bubble gum cards. You know, they grew up and I grew up at the same time. It's very exciting.

I think I'm not going to like being middle-aged. I think the worst that could happen is for me to be simply a housewife. Actually, my generation just doesn't think in those terms anymore. You can't have the suburban, *Trouble in Tahiti* thing happening with this generation. They just won't stand for it. They don't want boredom. As for me, I just can't wait to see what's going to happen. I just can't wait! **99**

17. The villa kitchen is brimming with activity. Maestro Bernstein's birthday party this evening will include a supper for some twenty guests. The preparations are more elaborate than usual. Everyone is busy at some task and the entire villa resounds with the voices of the servants seeing to it that everything will look and taste just right.

Lenny is in his studio practicing the piano part of a Hummel chamber work which he will play at the Philharmonic's 125th anniversary concert in the winter. The piece is florid and difficult: Lenny works and reworks certain phrases. He stops. Begins again. The intricacies are mastered. The runs are clear and brilliant. There are filigree passages that Lenny repeats again and again. The practicing lasts a long while. Finally, Lenny emerges from his study, dressed in a bathing suit. He invites me to join him for a swim.

"That Hummel stole from everyone! Beethoven, Donizetti, Chopin—it's a mad piece, but such fun!" I tell Lenny about my marvelous conversation with Jamie. We talk about the children. I am curious about his early relationship with his own brother and sister. And I learn that because of the lack of closeness with his parents, Lenny's affections turned to his sister Shirley, six years his junior. "We became very close and still are," he says. "It was a wonderful thing for us." When she graduated from Mount Holyoke, Lenny was already living in New York and she decided to come, too. He was then writing *On the Town* and she enlisted in the cast, in the chorus, and that's how her life began in New York.

"When she first came," Lenny says, "we shared an apartment on 55th Street. She also toured with me. She went to Europe with me. She went to Pittsburgh with me when *Jeremiah* was first done. She went to Israel with me the first time I went. So her life was constantly bound up with mine."

Burton Bernstein was born when Lenny was thirteen. Despite this gap in their ages, they too became very close. When Burton was in his teens the brothers made frequent trips together. And when Lenny was at Tanglewood, Burton came to assist in the Opera Department.

"When the three of us are together it's a perfect cosmos," Lenny continues, "which isn't good for any of us, but there it is and it's beautiful. We have so many private jokes and references."

Rybernia, for one. Rybernia is a mythical country that Lenny and his friend Eddie Ryack invented when they were about twelve. It is composed of syllables from the two names. There was a language, a national anthem, and rites of initiation. It's a language Shirley, Burtie, and Lenny still employ.

We are now back on the terrace having a late afternoon drink. The swim has refreshed and invigorated Lenny. As the summer has progressed, his back has given him less and less trouble. He looks very young and I tell him so. "I suppose there are various things that keep one youthful," he says. "Talking about Shirley and Burtie during our youth. One's own children and, maybe, a basically youthful attitude or spirit. Even my despair is youthful, in the sense that I don't ever get into that state apropos of being old, or of death. I have no particular fear of death or anxiety about it.

"I suppose in some ways you could call me not youthful, but childish. When my siblings and I indulge in Rybernian reminiscence, I am being childish, not youthful. Yet there always has been great joy—insane, ecstatic joy, moments of drunkenness—caused merely by being together and having these insanely funny jokes in common.

"Another thing that's useful about my rela-

tionship with Shirley and Burtie is that they bring me down constantly. It's part of the fun. There are very familiar, well-established taunts and teases about, say, not being taller. Shirley is always referred to in equine terms by us. In fact, we call her 'Horse.' It's one of her nicknames. If she stubs her toe, we talk of it as her 'hurting her fetlock.' There are wild put-downs which keep us all down to earth, but mainly me, because in their minds I'm the one in danger of going off to Cloud 9, in a great euphoric haze of egomania. They see to it—as do my children and wife—that I don't, by constantly puncturing the balloon that may carry me thither.

"My brother and sister are very loving— and very proud. It's just that they're irreverent, which is at it should be. I wouldn't have it any other way."

Shirley Bernstein lives in New York, in the apartment on West 55th Street she once shared with Lenny. She works as an executive at Ashley-Famous, a large talent agency. Shirley Bernstein has an electric energy, very much akin to Lenny's. She exudes vitality, she is articulate, she is dynamic, she is funny. She is attractive. Vis-à-vis her brother, Shirley emerges as a person imbued with contradictory feelings and vulnerabilities. Lenny has affected her life deeply. We talked about it, upon my return from Italy.

❝ Until I was about eight I was the pesty kid sister (she told me), but then we became friends. That's when music began between us. We were singing whole operas by the time I was ten. Of course, I had taken piano lessons, as kids do, and I was very talented, but the competition was getting impossible. I mean, when you're hammering out baby exercises and he is beating out the Grieg Concerto, it becomes impossible. I asked to be allowed to stop, which my mother couldn't wait to agree to.

But I had learned how to read notes, and under Lenny's stern tutelage I learned to fake at the piano, especially when he dragged out the Beethoven symphonies. I remember we had Volume II, Symphonies Six through Nine. And we played them. Of course, the scherzo movements we played lento. But we played great second movements and usually could blunder through a first. But he would keep me up at night—this little child—and hit me, *hit* me, saying, "Wrong! That's wrong!" Of course, I was adoring it. Mother would scream about the racket and about being kept up to all hours.

Then came the opera period. Lenny would come home with *Aida,* or whatever, and teach it to me. I had this pretty little soprano voice, and he'd be all the boys and I'd be all the girls and we'd both be the chorus. Of course, I got nodes on my throat; that's why I now sing baritone. But when that happened, when I was about fifteen, I began to sing blues; I had a natural blues sound. And we got out Bessie Smith and Billie Holiday records. But I can't sing opera anymore, which is very sad because I loved it so.

Anyway, Lenny taught me an enormous lot about music. And when I was in my early teens we began to have talks. He broadened my horizons enormously. Even then he began to teach me and open the way for my understanding of people, and to inspire me to be curious about things of the mind, and about the world. The result of all this was that he was the one I always wanted to please, not so much my father or my mother. It was much more important that I please Lenny, because he was the one who'd say "good" or "bad," and because he had been the teacher. He was a surrogate father in a funny way.

But, as I say, we became friends and had great fun together. Such fun and such laughter and gaiety. By the time he got to college—he was sixteen—I saw him less, because he was home only on weekends. And I was busy growing up myself.

Later, when I started going out with boys my age, I found that they seemed awfully childish. They couldn't discuss with me the things that Lenny could. We couldn't make music together, couldn't have the same kind of laughter. Kids my own age were talking about baseball, and flirting, and pushing each other a lot. I remember the big sign of affection used to be that they pushed you.

I was always torn. Of course, on one level I enjoyed them, and in the college years the romances came, and all that. But they never compared with my relationship with Lenny. And that was a kind of a curse, because none of the boys, no matter how bright or how darling or how whatever, had his mental capacities or ways of looking at things.

I remember thinking in college—I had just broken off a big romance—I was trying to figure out in my very young, sixteen-year-old way why this had happened. I remember realizing that I had an unconscious rule that I invoked with every boy I met. That if within, say, three days, I didn't have the emotional intimacy I had with Lenny, I'd reject the person.

I didn't realize all this very clearly. That happened when I was much older. I suddenly realized that I demanded of brand new relationships the same things that I had from years of relationship with my brother. The day I realized this was a very shocking day, because it suddenly seemed impossible ever to achieve it.

It was an enormous hindrance to my growing up, because even if Lenny weren't so talented and such a special figure, even if it were only the very warm, intimate, brother-and-sister relationship—this would be bad enough. But when you added all the rest of it—the mind and the talent—it was insurmountable. What guy could compete with that?

The fellows took one of two ways: Either they became very aggressive, to compete—or, after a while, realized there was no competing and just went away. I never coped very well with this, because the demands I made—without realizing it—were too great. What I was saying to them silently was, "Why aren't you as smart? Why aren't you as much fun to be with? Why can't I relax with you? Why is there no ease? Why don't we have secret jokes?"

The curse of it, of course, is that most people never have such an intimate relationship in their lives. You're very lucky to have it with anybody. But if you want every relationship to measure up to it, it's not possible. So you ask me how Lenny has affected me. He has affected me very strongly.

The men I've liked best in my life, if I analyze it very closely—something about them reminds me of Lenny. I mean they don't have to look anything like him, but there is some quality, some energy, an internal energy, a creative thing, that attracts me to them.

Burtie was my kid brother. Lenny was my big brother. That's very different. Burtie was, again, a pesty kid until he was fifteen. Then he joined us. At Tanglewood, I remember, the three of us were walking with arms around each other across the green, which we did all the time. But on one particular day we felt terribly together. And that evening someone alluded to the impregnable Bernstein Front.

As for my working with Lenny, well, first of all we are all supersensitive about nepotism to a degree that's perhaps foolish. But then, when Lenny was doing *On the Town* he suggested I be in the chorus. I hadn't even thought about it. And he said, "Look why don't you audition for George Abbott, like everybody else?"

Of course, it wasn't exactly like everybody else, truthfully, because after all what was George Abbott going to say, unless I was absolutely croaking? But at the time I had to justify it to myself, and I had to go through this ghastly audition, except that Lenny played for me. Anyway, when I got through George said, "Of course, why not?"

Luckily, it was the kind of a show that didn't demand great skill from a member of the chorus. So there it was. My one professional involvement with Lenny. Although, I must say I never quite lost my self-consciousness about a show my brother had written the music for. I never had any illusions about my talent. I knew I had a certain amount of it and that it didn't belong in the chorus. On the other hand, it wasn't "star time" either. Ultimately, I couldn't fool myself. You need to think you're the greatest thing on earth to go through that. And you've got to believe in yourself so. I knew better. I know I was a very minor talent. Also, I didn't like the life—sleeping all day and up all night.

So, after *On the Town* I did a bit of summer stock and then I said, "Enough is enough," and I stopped. I got a job as assistant to a producer, John Houseman, and began to learn a tremendous lot. He is a very erudite man, a marvelous, witty, amusing man, and he was my mentor. After that, I started to make my way in a rough profession—producing.

Lenny now? I think he's a deeply frustrated man because of the composing. The conducting and composing syndrome in Lenny is completely reflective of the split of his personality. The inward Lenny is the composer—the man who must be alone and fiddle with an F-sharp for hours. For me this is the most interesting part of Lenny. It's the Lenny I feel closest to, love the most.

The other part of him is the performer side —the outgoing side, the party side, which is perfectly fine and dandy, but it's that part of him I feel much less close to. There is only one quality in Lenny that he doesn't seem to know is really impossible. That is the kind of unconscious gaffe he makes that walks right into the most vulnerable place in somebody.

Many people have said to me that the one thing they've noticed is that when Lenny enters a room its temperature changes. He's one of those people. I mean, it changes either for good or for bad. Everybody reacts strongly. Hating him, loving him, envying him—something! It's extraordinary. I've seen this many times. He changes the climate of a room. People who don't know better look at you as though you are mad if you say that there is something shy in him, something unsure, and in need of love. But, my God, it's so true! "

Shirley Bernstein is articulate about her brother. Burton Bernstein, who is articulate on any number of other subjects, prefers to be relatively inarticulate about Lenny. Throughout the summer in Italy, he and Lenny spent many hours together. But they were hours, not days. Burton Bernstein leads his own life. All the Bernsteins call him Burtie, or equally often, B.B. He is taller and thinner than Lenny, with a lithe, athletic build and a face that echoes Lenny's in structure, though not in intensity. His eyes are pale green. He is soft-spoken and in many ways the antithesis of Lenny.

During the summer, he kept postponing a promised chat about Lenny. Finally he agreed to make a date with me—a date which fell on the very day Lenny, Felicia, and I landed in Sardinia. In the haste and spontaneousness of our trip, I forgot our date and I was of course aghast. But when we returned, and I had made elaborate apologies which he good-naturedly accepted, he agreed to have lunch at my villa.

"I'm much more puritanical than my brother," he told me. "I'm much more bourgeois. I'm not an exhibitionist and I don't like making speeches. I certainly don't want to be as famous as Lenny. It leaves you so little freedom."

Burtie is a writer, the author of two published books, *The Grove* and *The Lost Art*. He is also on the staff of *The New Yorker* magazine. He went to Dartmouth and to graduate school at Columbia. At the age of fourteen, he fell in love with airplanes and became the youngest licensed pilot in America. Lenny taught Burtie how to play tennis, but as Burtie put it, "the minute I started to beat him, he became furious. But we are very close and we were even closer when the three of us were much younger. We shared everything and had great fun. It was all a great lark. We had our own mythology, our own secret rites, our own arcane private jokes. I suppose our great closeness was created by the fact that our parents are so markedly of another generation. In retrospect, my father's early attitude toward Lenny and his music seems rather sensible to me. After all, he could not foresee Lenny's future, and he only wanted the best for his son.

"As a musician and as a conductor, Lenny has produced a precedent. I mean, an American kid can now grow up and become Leonard Bernstein. His greatest contribution, I think, is education. Almost singlehandedly, through TV, Lenny has brought music into the living room. He's a household word. And he's so American, so thoroughly American. Lenny loves his fame. He loves being in the spotlight. He loves cutting a good figure. He's a brilliant conductor, and his ten years at the Philharmonic have, after all, been the longest reign of any conductor with that orchestra."

Burton Bernstein is a diffident man. He is cautious and does not relish discussing Lenny for hours on end. One feels his private identity must be preserved at all costs. As a youngster he remembers being patted on the head by countless people, all delivering more or less the same line: "Are you going to become a musician like your brother?" It's a line he has learned to flee from. He is his own man. Burton, his wife Ellen (an interesting and highly attractive girl of Dutch origin), and their two small children, Karen and Michael, form a nucleus away from the Leonard Bernstein aura of wealth and success. They move among writers in a more muted world where privacy and solitude are taken for granted.

Lenny adores his brother Burtie, grows wistful over him, feels like a father toward him. When they are together the jokes and the allusions tend to stem from the past. But always one senses the affection between them, a great tie that sustains their closeness despite the complexities and psychological burdens they share.

As Shirley puts it, "Somewhere Burtie has shut off in himself the very motors that have always propelled Lenny. He has done this out of choice, I believe.

To be Burton Bernstein, private person, is what matters most to him.

18. Burtie, his wife Ellen, Donald Stewart and his wife Luisa, the Eric Smiths from London, and a dozen or more acquaintances made during the summer arrive for Lenny's birthday party. Felicia, the children, and Lenny receive their guests with warm handshakes, hugs, or kisses.

Tables have been set up on the terrace. It is a calm, warm evening, and people sit or stand making conversation—discussing the coming end of the summer, looking back and looking forward, wondering where the time has gone. Then the evening centers on Lenny and his forty-ninth birthday.

Gifts are brought and immediately opened. A painting of the children from Felicia. Many of the other presents are jokes—mad collages with "in" references to Lenny's likes and dislikes, several poems on the same order. Lenny proffers exclamations of pleasure, surprise, and explosive laughter. The drinks are generous and the dinner delicious. Birthday telegrams have arrived all day in fat bunches. Most of these are read aloud during dinner, eliciting applause and funny comments.

After dinner, Jamie, Alexander, and Nina prepare the children's games. Chairs are set up for musical chairs. Felicia mans the record player, choosing a recording of tangos for the game. Great hilarity as we all join in, moving cautiously then frantically around the chairs. Lenny wins at musical chairs. Next comes spin-the-bottle. More hilarity, giggles, and, of course, kisses. It is all great fun.

The night draws on. Some of us dance. More conversation, more laughter, more drinks. Through it all, Lenny is charming and funny. There is much tenderness for him, much embracing and much warmth. But imperceptibly a private sadness comes over him. He does not fall into a sudden gloom, but as it gets later, and as the guests begin to leave, there is something quite melancholy about him.

When everyone has left, he stands by himself on the terrace. Felicia, exhausted from the day and the party, gives Lenny a hug, then goes to bed. The children have already retired. Although he is somber and quiet, Lenny does not seem fatigued. "Why don't we fix ourselves one last drink," he tells me. "A nightcap." We sit down and we talk. It will be our last extended conversation of the summer and I decide to tape it. What follows, then, is a transcript of the actual dialogue, with all its brilliant moments, late-evening blurriness, and sudden insights:

J. G.: Is music where it should be?

L. B.: I don't think it *isn't* where it should be. But this is one of those periods when things seem to be coming to an end. The signs have been so clear for so long about the diminution of creativity—even in the great flurry of creation that goes on. I suppose there have never been so many composers alive in the world as there are now, or so many performances of their music, or so many performers, so many orchestras, so many outlets, so much audience, so many recordings.

J. G.: And yet?

L. B.: And yet I have this awful feeling that there is an inverse proportion between creation and creativity, between what is created and the creativeness of it.

J. G.: How so?

L. B.: Well, it all ties up with my almost Spenglerian feeling about the decline of Western man, or of Faustian man, as we have known him for several thousands of years. Twenty-five hundred years, let's say, of glorious culture, which seems to be grinding to a halt except, of course, scientifically. Somehow our philosophic and creative and artistic motors are not functioning on a par with our scientific ones—which is certainly not an original thought of mine, but one you can read in any Sunday rotogravure section—accounting for the moral lapse, for the various gaps that we find in our culture.

J. G.: And is it not true that the scientific explosion is backed up by tremendous money and the arts don't get anything like the same degree of support?

L. B.: Indeed. Science is backed by military greed. That is exactly the sign of decline—that our energy, which in our civilization means money, is thrown mainly into a scientific competition with other nation-states. The other night at dinner something like this came up— some theory of the universe that Alexander was expounding. Jamie said, "When it all ends...." I said, "You say that so coolly. Do you really expect it to end? Are you ready for it?" And she said, "You see, we weren't around during World War II. We don't know about that. So we have no points of reference. We don't have anything to remember, like desolation, destruction, despair. For us the idea of World War III or the end of the world is an abstract idea. I've had a very good life up till now." "And everybody has to die sometime," said Alexander, "and we're ready." There they sat, smiling happily—two charming children who adore life—and are as cool as cucumbers when they talk about the end of the world. It's as though they sense it. It's an awful thing to talk about, because whatever you do is poisoned by this feeling, or by this conviction.

J. G.: There has suddenly seeped into the unconscious of people a sense of great depression, which hovers over the most creative persons, and it seems that whatever they are doing is somewhat colored by this unknown something that spells The End.

L. B.: I know it's true of me. I tend to be very enthusiastic; I can get terribly involved in what I'm doing; and I find that even with me this is true. Last month, in Israel, which—this minute—is one of the most inspiring places to be in the world, I kept thinking, "For what? Why are they breaking their heads against this wall?" I had this feeling of slight depression, even in the midst of this elation and euphoria on top of Mt. Scopus in Jerusalem. I know Felicia has it enormously.

J. G.: I know. It's all-pervasive.

L. B.: I have one or two saving factors. I love music so much that it keeps me glued to life, even when I'm most depressed. I still have the capacity for work, and that saves me. The other thing is people. I can't believe that people can let themselves be drawn into such a trap. Man can't be just a poor trapped animal, victim of his own greeds and diplomatic follies and aggression. Either one believes there is this divine element in man, or one doesn't. So as long as I believe it—which is, I suppose, what makes me love people—then I have to hope in some remote corner of my soul that there is a way out.

J. G.: Why is it that high-ranking politicians seldom talk about the divinity of man?

L. B.: No. I think anything pertaining to divinity is used as a kind of shibboleth. It's a thing to go to war by, to preach by, to give the okay-to-policy by. Forward for God and King Harry, you know. But I also think that statesmen, so-called, become so incredibly caught up in the details of their statesmanship. Because, after all, they are dealing with power. It somehow doesn't leave them room or time to sense the big things.

J. G.: What possible solution is there?

L. B.: I've been through them all. I've run out of solutions. There have been days and weeks when I have thought that the only saving factor was in art.

J. G.: Do you still feel that?

L. B.: No. Not today. I've been appalled, for

example, at the lack of any artistic voice in the present crisis, in the conflicts of crises that we've been going through with Vietnam, the Negroes, human rights, civil rights.

J. G.: But in what way?

L. B.: I mean, in works of art. The best works of art are works of despair now. What are the plays that are interesting just now? The plays of Pinter, Beckett—these are plays of despair. The music that is good is of despair. It's fragmented, it's atomized. It's very hard to find a work of art about which the word nobility can be used anymore. Ever since 1945 the face of art has become cool, hip, put-on, campy. Everything except hopeful, noble. Those things were sort of relegated to Soviet tractor-art, which you and I have laughed at along with the rest of Western society. The last noble strains we heard were Shostakovich's Fifth or Seventh Symphonies.

J. G.: It must be because people can't believe in that any longer.

L. B.: I can't believe you're right.

J. G.: Well, the young artists can't believe it because all that nobility has done nothing, except bring about destruction anyway. That's why they are pooh-poohing everything and making an art out of trivia. It's a kind of trivia that's directed at the world in general, not against art itself. And against the perceiver.

L. B.: Yes. It's against the audience, the gallery-goer.

J. G.: It is even against themselves, so that they themselves might then be safe and not have any fingers pointed at them.

L. B.: Also it's against themselves as lovers of art.

J. G.: What they don't seem to realize, of course, is that this brings on its own set of conventions.

L. B.: But what about an enormous talent, like our friend Larry Rivers? Let's say he attempts something as vast and monumental as the "History of the Russian Revolution," which is an extremely impressive piece of goods. Let's say it's one of the more monumental things that have been created in the last two years in our country. But what does it amount to? One admires it, one is amused by it, certainly, because it has all these surprises in it. But then what? Is one moved by it? Is one ennobled, enriched by it?

J. G.: Well, one is dazzled by it. Larry has an extraordinary capacity for telescoping a movement, for taking the whole shebang and putting it in one work, and there you have it. He combines Pop, nostalgia, and the political. All of these things are incorporated and—miraculously—it works. One may not be moved, but he has shown us something almost in retrospect. He has brought something forward, perhaps a commentary on art.

L. B.: Well, then, let's say that today the function of art has changed. That one is not supposed to be enriched or ennobled by it, not moved or exalted by it. But what is that a sign of?

J. G.: Yet people seem still to be ennobled by a performance of great music. I know I still am moved, and I know that hundreds of thousands of people still are moved by the art of the past.

L. B.: That I know. *That* we haven't lost. The past. But that's not what we're talking about.

J. G.: No. But those who create today can be moved and ennobled by works of the past. I know Larry is, for example. He can look at a Delacroix, or any great painter, and be moved. Of course, that does not necessarily mean he is about to move people by his own work. So what I'm saying is that they themselves can no longer capture the feeling that they themselves experience.

L. B.: Are you moved by the poetry of Robert Lowell?

J. G.: Sometimes. Somehow, being moved implies that the thought processes involving understanding the poem—you know, the great arrow that wavers between understanding meaning and how the meaning is created. There is this constant battle between the craft of it and the thought and meaning that is produced by it.

L. B.: Well, I admire it enormously, which is why I bring it up. But I am never moved. What I'm trying to get at is: What can one be moved by now? Forget the movies for a minute.

J. G.: I think today one is moved more by people than by art.

L. B.: Well, do you think there is a possibility that with the civilization of the world—if such a thing is possible, if we can survive these crises and the growing up of man—that art becomes less and less necessary? I mean, if art always arises from a sense of struggle, need, conflict, lack in some area which is supplanted by the artistic experience, and these needs are taken care of by social and evolutionary advancement, then art disappears. But even that would be a hopeful sign, because at least the disappearance of art would not be an indication of the imminent demise of man, which it seems to be. I'm pretty sure that if a complete evolution were possible, and every problem were solved, and man found ways of rectifying everything that was wrong—of supplying all his needs by varying capsules and rays and electronic means—that he might very well not need art anymore. Can you conceive of what a world that would be? Is that a world you'd like to live in? Doesn't it sound rather sterile? All right. Then take it a step further. Doesn't it mean, then, that we are addicted to our problems? In some sort of masochistic way, we love having them? And we are addicted to having art to make us feel better? And to suffer by?

J. G.: Yes. We have an infinite desire to be troubled and have a means of escape through art, except that art is falling away. Still, I believe art will always be with us, even if it's only a means of purging ourselves. I think you must embark on a new project—an opera....

L. B.: Why?

J. G.: Because it will still help people be transported.

L. B.: It's a rather poor arrangement, when you come to think about it. Isn't it? That man is so constituted that he has to suffer in this vale of tears, and then comes to like his suffering through art. I mean, that wouldn't stand up for a minute in a scientific laboratory. But that's what we have. An extremely imperfect design which is saved, I must repeat, only by this divine spark of intelligence which gives one hope that he can go on improving his own design. So you wish me to become a party to this whole conspiracy, or game, by providing yet more works of art by which people can re-experience their suffering and be granted a catharsis thereby. It doesn't really seem to be improving the lot of mankind as much as it is contributing to the status quo.

J. G.: Yes. But I have the feeling that the more you show the suffering, hopefully, the more compassion is engendered. And that is something positive. One wants, then, to be good.

L. B.: What we've really been talking about is the function of art—and you were saying to me that I must run upstairs and write my pieces quick, quick, quick. I've been saying, "Why?" And you say, because ultimately it will help people. Help them how? Get through? Survive? Engender compassion? That's simply keeping the same ball rolling.

J. G.: Well, it will make them pause, momentarily, for reflection.

L. B.: Do they really need another work by me? Another hundred works by another hundred me's? Do they? This is one of those critical moments in history, it seems to me, when either world civilization is going to shoot forward in some tremendous way, or stop. I don't think it can hang on this way anymore. That's what I mean by the Spenglerian decline. You see, it's not that all is lost, but that some mutation must take place in human behavior, in human psychology.

J. G.: But getting back to, let's say, our need for *your* continuing to write. An enormous number of people listen to you. You have a vast audience. And since people not only listen to you conduct, and listen to your music, but also love you as a man, who knows that you shouldn't actually speak to them—talk to them, I mean—address them.

L. B.: If I had any really deep convictions at this moment I think I *would* speak. But I've gotten to the point where I feel I know nothing. I know absolutely nothing. I have moments when I hope for some glorious sudden spurt that'll save us. Or there are moments when I just want to take people and shake them and say, "Come to your senses and stop this." But I can't. That is not my function. I am not a political man. In the generic sense, I am, of course, a political man. But I'm not in politics. I don't crave that sort of authority. You see, what the present crisis really boils down to is not only a crisis in faith. It is more basic. It's the greatest in a series of crises. It's a crisis of world revolution which has been going on for thousands of years, and has accelerated. This revolution is based on the right to eat. And we of the West, who insist on the right to eat at other people's expense, seem to be doing everything we know to prevent this revolution from taking place. Instead of aiding it, and making it happen in a positive way, lending our money and power, we are using our money and power to prevent its happening. The United States as a nation, as an entity, seems to be totally dedicated to that task, under the title of "Preserving Our Way of Life." And our way of life just isn't good enough. It just is not humanitarian enough. It seems to me that that divine spark of intelligence which I keep alluding to hopefully would show us that, so that the democracy we boast of might be able to function in another way, not as an enemy of the revolution. After all, we were created in revolution. We made it up. We're so proud of it! Why is it we are always supporting the wrong side?

J. G.: Have you not spoken privately about such matters to important people? To people who have power? What are the answers?

L. B.: Oh, well, it always winds up with their saying, "These things are so complicated." And they are, of course. But they seem to let the complexities screen off the basic, blinding, simple truths. I remember talking to President Kennedy in the White House, one night—this was in 1962 or early 1963—and I was terribly worried about the Vietnamese situation. I asked him what we were doing there. He said he would give *anything* not to be in Southeast Asia. He said it was a thing he had inherited from the previous Administration, that he was stuck with it. I said there must be something he could do about it. He said he didn't know what. This coming from him—of all political men that I have ever met certainly the most moving and compassionate and lovable, and the one to whom most of us turned in trust and in hope. Of course, it's very easy to say now, "If he had lived...." But I think the signs, when you look at them coldly, in a harsh, clear light, point to his having followed the same pattern being followed now, because he did actually order increased troops and escalation. He was stuck with it. I don't know what he could have done. That night, when we talked, he had no answers. He was in a kind of despair himself.

J. G.: Did he wish to change the course of events?

L. B.: Yes. He desperately wanted peace. But then the complexities set in. Face-saving. Power politics. Being accused of being an appeaser. Soft on Communism. Attacked by his Congress and by the majority of the country. It's horrible. It's as though he were a slave, instead of a leader.

J. G.: Let's get back to you. How much do you believe in yourself as a composer?

L. B.: You are bringing up a very complicated thing. You see, one so envies people of the past who knew what they were about, or who understood what their functions were.

J. G.: Really? I don't truly believe they always did understand.

L. B.: You don't believe that Bach was convinced that everything he wrote was in the service and in the praise of God? But, of course! He was an absolutely coordinated and integrated man. He had problems, I'm sure. But not of the kind we're talking about. His function was known to him. His reason for doing whatever he did was never questioned for a moment.

J. G.: Yes. But that was all very much simpler to do in those days. It was a taken-for-granted attitude. It was almost automatic.

L. B.: Well, all right. But let's take Schumann and Berlioz, or Wagner. They were just as unquestioning and secure in their faith that what they were doing was in the interests of art, and that the artist had the message. It was a kind of substitute religion.

J. G.: But that was because they were not being torn or fractionalized by the society in which they lived. I'm sure they would not be so convinced of their messages were they alive today. Given *your* sensitivity, intelligence, and inquisitiveness, you could not possibly be con-vinced of your art. In a way, they were wearing blinders and you are not.

L. B.: How wonderful to have been that simple. Living in the world I live in makes me less of an artist.

J. G.: I don't know about that.

L. B.: Oh, I do! I think absolutely so. You see, to believe in yourself means that you have some sort of blinders on. You find it very difficult to concentrate on anything more than whatever it is you do. And maybe a little bit on what your competitors do, a little bit on what the critics say you do, and a little bit on how the public reacts to what you do. Believing in oneself means believing in one's function—believing completely in the work one does—as being absolutely and inextricably woven with the destiny of the world, of being essential, all-important. It involves a certain egomania, which all good artists have, which I've been accused of having, and which I find I don't have enough of, really. On the contrary. I suffer from the lack of egomania. Because if I had it to the degree that I think it's necessary to have it as an artist, I wouldn't be questioning anything. If you said to me, "What's important?" I would say, "I'm important because of what I do and what I'm contributing to the world, for whatever reason." But I find it increasingly difficult to think in those terms. I'm sure that when I was in my twenties I felt that way, that the sun rose and set on my coming and going. The painful process of growing up is simply the constant ever-widening realization that you are not the center. It's painful. That's why adolescence is painful. Maturing is a painful process. I suppose that most great artists don't really mature as people. They retain something of that infantile self-centeredness which makes them think of themselves as the fulcrum. Everything may be very important, but it's ancillary

Text continues on page 166

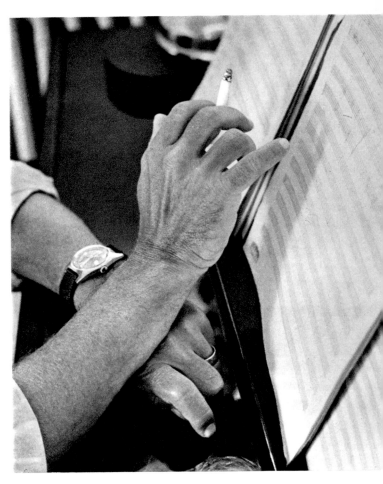

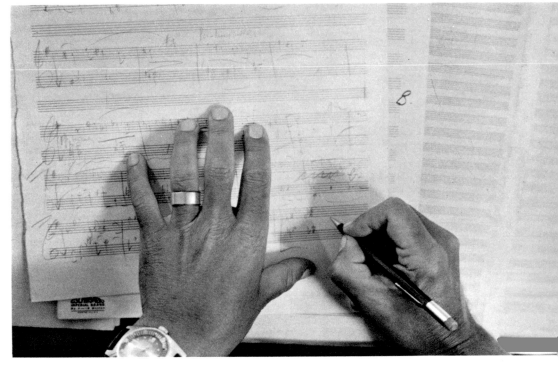

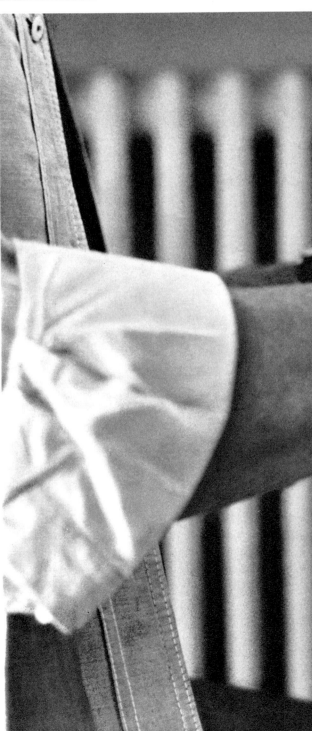

Continued from page 154

and incidental to this main thing which is Me, and what I'm doing. At the moment I am weak in the conviction that to compose is of any importance to me or to anybody else.

J. G.: Is it because you have reached a certain pinnacle of acclaim, or fame, or adulation? Is it because you are sated with praise and that you don't have to struggle any longer to make your fame and fortune? Has this made you lose your conviction?

L. B.: Absolutely not. I can never be sated with praise and adulation because it doesn't stay with me. I mean, it's not that important. It goes through a sieve and runs out. It's lovely while it happens. I wouldn't dream of playing Mr. Modest. I'm saying it doesn't affect me. I love it. Who doesn't? But then it's gone.

J. G.: And what are you left with?

L. B.: Well, you're left with what is real. What's real is your work and your own evaluation of it. Your satisfaction or lack of it.

J. G.: Let's turn to the style of your work. Are you still, in effect, in search of a style? Are you dissatisfied with the style in which you now compose?

L. B.: That's a practical point to bring up. Having been wrapped up so much of the last ten years in the New York Philharmonic, which means almost constant conducting, the intervals of time available to me have never been enough to get going again as a composer. As a result of these long gaps between composing periods—and even longer gaps between one piece and the next—it has been very difficult for me to evolve what you call a style, a language I'm always speaking, always enlarging, enriching, changing by simply speaking in it all the time which is the way languages remain living. When people criticize my music as being eclectic, they are right. It is. It always has been eclectic and probably always will be. For this reason. Also for other reasons. But I

think no music has ever been written that wasn't eclectic, that hasn't been dependent on music which preceded it. This is as true of Mozart and Brahms as it is of Monteverdi and Stravinsky. But whatever influences you detect —whatever combinations of other styles one can find, say, in a Beethoven piano sonata— there is with it that incredible individual voice which is always recognizable, always there. If I have that to any degree at all at this point, it's a miracle. I hope, certainly, to have it more as I go on composing. But this will happen when composing is a more continuous and consistent activity. You see, it is two years since I wrote my last note, the *Chichester Psalms.* Since June, 1965, I have not been able to begin to form a composition. You now find me— August 25, 1967—in the position of starting all over again from where I was then! It's very difficult. I mean the muscles that were all exercised then and ready for use have now gone slack. I don't know where to begin. I pick up a pencil and think, "Now what do you do when you write a piece? What do you do first?" It's as though I had never done it before. I have to begin again. Each piece I've written has been like that. There were two years between *Kaddish* and the *Psalms.* There were six years between *West Side Story* and *Kaddish.* Absolutely nothing in between! Six years! I'm told that I have a personal voice in my music. Thank God for that. If I believed that there wasn't a voice, I don't think I would ever write music. But it's very difficult to pick up the pieces. This, of course, militates against having a very strong, individual style. So, naturally, my music will always be eclectic to a certain degree. I don't care, if that small voice is still there.

J. G.: Do you think you might ever embark on writing atonal music?

L. B.: No. That's not in my cards. I've fooled

around with it. I tried during my sabbatical year, and I reported on it. I spent about two months experimenting with various kinds of nontypical styles. But I threw it all away and wrote the *Chichester Psalms,* which is about the most tonal and baby-simple piece I've ever written. No. I still think the hardest thing for a composer to do in our time is to write a tonal melodic line that doesn't sound stale. That is why I'm very proud of those *Psalms.* They contain utterly diatonic phrases which, at least to me, sound fresh and moving. That is a great accomplishment for me. I don't have to go and meddle in electronic or serial music in order to satisfy my longing for advancement and originality. I don't think that is the way I can advance music.

We have talked far into the night. Lenny becomes aware of this and quickly shifts into a retrospective mood about the ending summer in Ansedonia. "I may now have a nice, healthy glow about me," he says, "but I don't have a nice healthy *inner* glow. I suppose I did a lot of things this summer, despite it all: driving the Maserati, using the diving gear, the boat. But I couldn't fully enjoy them because of my back. I've done so little sightseeing. I haven't even been to Tarquinia, which is so unbelievably close!

"Still, we had our madcap trip to Sardinia, which was marvelous fun. Stopping that time in the mountains. I was really as happy as I've ever been. It was so peaceful! The air was something I'll never forget. And picking raspberries and not feeling rushed. And it was a beautiful time of day! And that nice man who operated the barrier at the railway crossing, who invited us home with him!"

In this manner, Leonard Bernstein's Italian summer drew to a close. Felicia and he, the children and their maid Julia flew to New York on the first day of September. The mountains and the sea and the villa and all the summer thoughts slowly became echoes and memories growing more and more distant, more and more remote.

Mementos: With Helen Coates in office

19. Leonard Bernstein in New York. A vast change of tempo, a dizzying acceleration of activity. Bernstein is transformed. The public life takes over. Time is no longer his own. As director of the New York Philharmonic he is catapulted into a vast complex of duties, all of which he performs with extraordinary ease and assurance. Bernstein thrives under the pressures of a superhuman schedule.

A season usually begins with a four- to six-week tour with the orchestra. The 1967-68 season included a tour to Chicago, Ann Arbor, and various cities in Canada. In New York, Bernstein conducts the orchestra up to sixteen weeks. There are endless rehearsals. There are many sessions for Columbia Records. There are four telecasts of Young Peoples Concerts, which Bernstein conducts, hosts, and for which he writes the scripts. There are innumerable decisions which fall to Bernstein: choice of repertory, choice of soloists, approval of guest conductors. Even the Philharmonic's weekly program notes must be approved by Bernstein.

There is a vast correspondence which Bernstein attends to with the aid of his secretary Helen Coates. For a quarter of a century her life has been intertwined with Lenny's—ever since he came to her for piano lessons as a boy. It is perhaps the most remarkable of his many loyal long-term associations. "Lenny studied with me for three years," she says. "He was a very gifted boy and a very attractive boy —just fourteen he was—with personality just oozing out of him. I soon discovered you couldn't give Lenny just an hour lesson. He was so eager, so full of knowledge, and so eager for more.

"He's never practiced regularly, you know. Never in his whole life. He's not that kind. He'd always be prepared at the lesson—but it wasn't a question of so much practice every day. Of course he was always at the piano reading everything under the sun, but not practicing regularly. He told me that I taught him how to work. We kept in touch through the years. I had been teaching for a long, long time, and had been thinking of making a break. Lenny would say, 'Oh, Helen, if you'd only come down to New York and take over, I'm sure everything would be all right.' You see, things had become very hectic for him. He'd become tremendously active, and no one was there to sort of take care of things. So I began to think more and more about it, and finally I said I'd do it.

"What do I do? Well, in those early years I ran his apartment, I hired the help, planned the meals, did all the ordering. I packed Lenny whenever he went away, unpacked when he came home. Took care of all of his clothes. I was valet and I can't tell you what else. I took care of all of the business and correspondence. Since his appointment as director of the New York Philharmonic, I take care of all the phone calls that come in for him—except the personal ones—and I've always felt that the biggest part of my job for Lenny is public relations. Handling all these people on the telephone and having to say 'No' to so many things. That's been the hardest thing I've had to do all these years. Also, I handle all the correspondence. If he looked at all of his mail he'd have no time to do anything else. And the regular business mail! Lenny has no idea of the things I've turned down for him!

"I'm always in touch with his lawyer and his accountant. We consult on everything. I handle all the finances, except for the tax business. I do all the banking. I give Lenny all the cash he carries. Lenny doesn't want to be bothered with anything having to do with finances, doesn't want to hear about it. He will hardly glance at his financial record at the end of the year. Felicia has her own account and

New York: Entertaining friends.
Preceding pages (clockwise from top left):
Phyllis Newman Green, Jerome Robbins, Stephen
Sondheim, L. B., Robert Fizdale,
Cynthia O'Neal, Mrs. Fred Lazarus, Michael
Mindlin, Arthur Gold, John Gruen,
Jane Wilson Gruen, Ellen Oppenheim.
At right: With Phyllis Green and Mrs. Lazarus.
Below: With Jerome Robbins and Adolph Green.

checkbook, but that too comes to me and goes through my hands. I pay all the bills. I handle the payroll of all the servants and the caretaker in Fairfield—all of that.

"I have made a life for myself around Leonard Bernstein and it is very satisfying. I feel it's not only a great experience, but a wonderful privilege to be associated with such a person as Lenny and watch him grow as I have been privileged to do. Of course, I feel I'm probably the most privileged teacher I've ever heard about. I mean, for a teacher to have worked at that early age with a pupil, to have been closely associated all these years and involved in his professional life, as well—well, I've never heard of anybody who has ever had that privilege.

"I began collecting Bernstein memorabilia when I was still in Boston. The very first thing I pasted in that first clipping book was the story of a contest in which he missed winning a grand piano but got second prize. There was a picture of the contestants, and sitting in the middle of them all was little Lenny. From then on I started collecting and pasting everything in those books. And Lenny would collect things for me—programs and reviews—while on tour and I'd paste everything in. I remember when he was made assistant conductor of the New York Philharmonic, the *Herald Tribune* used a picture of Lenny with the announcement. He cut it out and wrote with a blue pencil on the margin, 'Here we go, Love, Lenny!' It was among the first things he sent me for the book. Now I have a clipping service—there are fifty-three volumes of clippings—but I still collect things myself. The bulk of the material is at the Library of Congress and the rest is on microfilm. It's an incredible record of Lenny's career. Then I have all kinds of awards—medals, scrolls, plaques—over at the Osborne in the rooms I call The Archives; all kinds of photographs; files and files of fan mail and correspondence and the press books.

"I've worked for Lenny for twenty-four years. I do have a personal life of my own, but my whole working life is with Lenny. And I have always put Lenny first, even above my personal life. I've always done that. I mean, my time is Lenny's first, no matter what else."

And so now in New York she assists him with the daily burden of administrative work. There are also meetings, conferences, luncheons. With Carlos Moseley, the Philharmonic's managing director, Bernstein confers on all matters pertaining to the orchestra. The expected and the unexpected are dealt with and gone into in greatest detail. Bernstein is the center around which the New York Philharmonic revolves. It is a life of consultations, decisions, and judgments. And it is, of course, a life of performing before the public.

But it is a life suitable to Bernstein's predisposition for doing many things at once—one that allows him to make use of his boundless energies.

When we returned from Italy, Bernstein immediately took off on his Philharmonic tour. Upon his return to New York, he plunged into the Philharmonic season, and then immediately into the Brecht theater project brought to him by Jerome Robbins. I called Bernstein upon his return to New York. Had his spirits improved now that he was back on his rigorous schedule? We made a date for after one of his Brecht sessions. Another late-hour interview.

I arrive at the Bernsteins' thirteen-room penthouse on Park Avenue. Lenny is still working. I hear the piano. I hear voices. A heated discussion is in progress.

While waiting for the session to conclude, I have a chance to talk with Felicia Bernstein. She tells me about accepting the role of Birdie in the Broadway run of *The Little Foxes* and that she has also signed for a seven-week tour with the play. Felicia is exhilarated by the prospect of being on the stage again. There is excitement in her voice as she tells me all about it. She looks beautiful—and is obviously happy about being back in New York. The summer, for all its change of pace and activity, had not been particularly happy for her. "Really, I'm thrilled to be back home. And so are the children, especially Jamie, who was really dying of loneliness in Ansedonia."

Felicia and Lenny at home. It is a complex household run by Felicia and a staff of three. The penthouse is a study in good taste and informality. Showiness or pretentiousness are decidedly avoided; all is geared to warmth, graciousness, ease, and comfort. The apartment centers on a large living room at one end of which stand two grand pianos. The room is beautifully proportioned, bright and airy during the daytime, cozily lit and subdued during the evening. It is handsomely furnished. The couches and easy chairs are upholstered in luxuriant floral patterns. There are many paintings, many books, many treasured objects, and fresh flowers, everywhere. There is a fireplace, and on the two pianos an array of photographs showing the Bernsteins alone, in family groups, with friends. Here Felicia and Lenny entertain. Parties are not regular occasions. But when they are given, they are lively and stimulating. There is much hilarity, a great deal of talk, and, occasionally, hours of music-making with Lenny at the piano.

The guests are usually old friends from many worlds: Betty Comden and her husband Steven Kyle, Adolph Green and his wife Phyllis Newman, Jerome Robbins, Mike Nichols, Samuel Barber, the Schuyler Chapins, Kitty Carlisle Hart, Gian-Carlo Menotti, the John Barry Ryans, Steve Sondheim, Lauren Bacall and Jason Robards, the Patrick O'Neals, the Mike Mindlins, Lillian Hellman, Larry and Clarice Rivers, actor George Segal and his wife, Michael Wager and his wife Susan, David and Ellen Oppenheim, Aaron Copland, Louis d'Almeida, Arthur Gold and Robert Fizdale, Jennie Tourel, the Richard Avedons, the Milton Greenes, the Lukas Fosses, the Goddard Liebersons. More often than not, Lenny's sister Shirley and his brother Burton and wife are present.

The mood is relaxed and convivial at these gatherings. Later food will be served in the dining room. This is a small, more intimate room. A mirrored table accommodates no more than eight people, some of whom sit on the deep-red velvet divan which forms an L around it. When the occasion demands, several smaller tables are set up. The company is treated to superb food prepared by a Chilean cook. There are excellent wines. The meal is eaten by candlelight. The atmosphere is quieter, more concentrated. The talk is more intense, more specific. It centers on political, theatrical, literary, and movie matters. Seldom on music. Discussion of people is high on the list of topics. Opinions and gossip are exchanged with a great deal of wit and humor. Through it all, Lenny and Felicia are responsive, attentive hosts. They exude vitality and charm. They have the ability to make a large party seem effortless.

After dinner, guests are invited into the library, where coffee and brandy are served. The library is the Bernstein's usual sitting room. Smaller than the living room, it too contains a fireplace, paintings, and hundreds of books. Hidden in one corner, behind a screen, are Felicia's easel and a work table.

Downstairs are the family bedrooms, the maid's rooms, and Lenny's studio, which is equipped with the accouterments of the composer and conductor. A piano dominates the

With parents: Mr. and Mrs. Samuel J. Bernstein

room. Piles of scores rest on top of it. Hundreds more line the bookcases. A desk, couch, coffee table all brim with books, letters, more scores, periodicals, newspapers, memorandums, notes. Shelves stacked with tapes, records, and test pressings line another wall. Hi-fi equipment is ever ready for use. A bath and shower adjoin Lenny's studio. It is here that he prepares before a concert.

The New York apartment is the center of the Bernsteins' activities. As a necessary respite from their hectic New York life, they retreat to their eighteen-acre country estate in Fairfield, Connecticut. The stately, white clapboard, ten-room farmhouse is kept open year round and is visited almost every weekend during the winter. It is usually occupied throughout the summer. Originally a salt-box, it gives the impression of having been added to sporadically through the years. To the rear stand several barn-red outbuildings: Lenny's studio, a large barn, unused stables, and the maid's cottage.

The grounds are spacious, rolling, beautifully tended, and informally planted. There is a large variety of trees, which are Felicia's pride and joy. Among the expected oaks and maples, are dogwood, a copper beech, a weeping beech, a tulip tree, a Japanese maple, and other exotic trees. There is a modest swimming pool, a tennis court, and many acres of woods with hidden springs.

Life in Connecticut is informal, peaceful, private. Felicia enjoys taking long walks in the woods, as, indeed, does everybody. The family comes to rest, to be together, and to be alone.

Lenny might shut himself up in his bright, spacious studio, standing for hours of work at a long, high desk. Felicia might paint, or read, or write letters. She and Jamie might sit and talk for hours about school, a particular problem that has arisen, or about growing up. Alexander might be with a classmate he's invited for the weekend. Little Nina will be everywhere, chattering, scurrying on the lawn, drawing pictures.

When all the Bernsteins are gathered in one room, they present a picture of familial unity and well-being. It is a very close family. The magnet that is Leonard Bernstein diminishes in this atmosphere. He is simply Daddy, or Ben, as Felicia often and inexplicably calls him. At these times, the mood is quiet. Lenny exclaims over a newspaper item. Jamie and Alexander work a picture-puzzle. Nina nestles in Felicia's lap, having a funny Nina-chat with Mummy. Whatever the strains, whatever the tensions, whatever the complexities to be found in the private world of Leonard Bernstein, none of these is apparent within the shared confines of this privateness.

And now Felicia and I sit over a drink in her New York living room. We talk about the summer, about the children, about the oncoming theater season, about Lenny's new project.

Suddenly, Lenny appears. He is flushed and somewhat tousled in appearance. The night's work has been exhausting but, obviously, exhilarating. He greets me with an embrace. He joins Felicia and me in a drink. In a little while he ushers me into his study.

"How is the Brecht going?" I ask him. "We're really still in the discussion stages," he tells me. "It's the kind of Brecht play that is extremely problematic to transfer to musical form unless you settle for writing songs in the Dessau or Weill traditions—and setting the lyrics that Brecht wrote, perhaps in some other translation or adaptation. That's a whole different kettle of beans. I wouldn't be particularly interested in that.

"I don't think Brecht's lyrics are very good;

also, the project wouldn't interest me except to musicalize it on a more elaborate basis than Brecht indicated. I don't mean that it should be elaborate. *The Exception and the Rule* is a very short and lean, biting, ironic play. So it shouldn't be a big thing. In fact, it's not going to be big in sound. It's not going to have any orchestra in the pit. The present plan is to have the company of players include musicians.

"I took it because I thought it would be a comparatively quick job. But it isn't. It's harder than *West Side Story*. I mean, how can we be funny about Brecht without seeming to put Brecht down? You mustn't kid the play at the same time that you're kidding around and trying to make it entertaining and funny. It's a very subtle and sharp line that has to be drawn. Every second has to be thought out. It's either too serious or too broad. You have to find the right, exact thing. I can't tell you what I've been through and thrown away. But it could be good, given enough time."

Bernstein pauses. He lights a cigarette. I learn that hours earlier he had received a telephone call from Boston informing him that his mother had been taken to the hospital with what seemed to be a heart attack. Both of his parents have heart trouble and this new crisis finds Lenny in a disquieted mood. As we talk he receives several calls from Boston, where his brother and sister had flown that morning. Both Shirley and Burtie inform him of their mother's progress. The following morning he would fly to Boston to be with his mother, who evidently made a satisfactory recovery.

Lenny looks at his calendar. He lets out a long breath. "I'm in a vise of panic for time. Between Christmas and New Year's (1968) is my week for looking at new scores. I conduct the whole month of January, and I've got to prepare all those scores. I have three world premieres to do, which I haven't begun to study, and a lot of other pieces I've never played before. Plus two television scripts! There are also two Young Peoples Concerts in that month. I've got to write those."

But it's all very typical. Bernstein's daily schedules are head-spinning affairs. No day passes but that Lenny is confronted with a barrage of appointments, meetings, conferences. He must attend to the expected and the unexpected. A typical day may begin with a rehearsal at ten. Michael, his English chauffeur and dresser, will have the black limousine ready and drive him to Philharmonic Hall. The rehearsal lasts for several arduous hours during which whole programs are shaped, focused, and polished. Wearing a tee-shirt and a towel around his neck, or a sweat-shirt, Bernstein digs deep into music he may perform that very evening.

To hear him speak to the men during rehearsals is to be in touch with a conductor obsessed with clarity. No one is more articulate than he in conveying meaning, mood, effect, or feeling, or in pursuing and pinpointing the musical, aesthetic, and psychological underpinnings of a piece of music. It's all done with utmost simplicity, often with humor, and always with enormous drive and intelligence. By now the men are totally responsive. They sense and frequently anticipate his every wish. Rehearsals or recording sessions are lessons in instinctive respect, understanding—and love. There are frantic moments, of course, difficult moments. Lenny can become angry. But most sessions run smoothly and become an engrossing act of musical concentration, immersion, and craftsmanship.

Rehearsal over, Bernstein is driven home. Dozens of phone messages await him. His agent, Robert Lantz, wishes to confer about requests and projects submitted, suggested, offered. His publishers have questions. Helen Coates calls in a message about an important appointment that has now been shifted to the following day. She herself is expected momentarily with correspondence that must be gone over. Jerry Robbins has called to set up a meeting on the Brecht. There are calls pertaining to the Philharmonic. John McClure, head of Columbia Records' classical division, has an urgent question that needs an immediate answer.

Even as he sits in his studio, the phones keep ringing. Michael materializes carrying armfuls of books and recordings that have just arrived for Bernstein. Felicia appears at the door to tell Lenny they had a call from an old friend in Vienna that morning, and that Alexander has put in a request for an hour's Hebrew lesson this afternoon after school. Helen Coates now arrives with stacks of mail. She reminds Lenny that a number of foreign dignitaries will be at the concert tonight and have asked to meet him afterwards. She hands him a list of their names. An hour is devoted to correspondence. Nina suddenly makes an entrance: "Hi, Daddy! I've learned to snap my fingers!" Then off she runs.

Through it all Lenny is alternately harassed, engrossed, tensely attentive, impatient, amused, bemused, exasperated, and always alert. Lenny is a man of detail. He asks detailed questions and expects detailed answers. His mind is fascinatingly retentive. Very little escapes his memory. Indeed, he has almost total recall. He absorbs, he stores, he recalls.

The hours fly. By midafternoon Bernstein will have made hundreds of decisions, answered quantities of mail, returned quantities of phone calls, answered quantities of questions. By now a nap is indicated, but Lenny has committed himself to a fitting by his tailor, who now appears and measures him for several new suits. Another hour goes by. Alexander now walks in armed with his Hebrew books. He and Lenny sit side by side on the studio couch and the lesson proceeds. It is an intense session and both emerge from it refreshed. Lenny no longer feels like napping.

The phones continue to ring. Jennie Tourel invites Lenny to attend one of her master classes at Carnegie Recital Hall. Lenny accepts and chats with Jennie for many minutes. There is much laughter. He adores her. Jamie walks in announcing that she's passed her French exam, and did he know that the Beatles' new album was FANTASTIC? The phones continue to ring. A call from London followed by a call from Paris. People in the music world requesting appearances, extracting promises.

Presently it is time to continue studying a new score he began looking at the previous day. The next two hours are devoted to that. Bernstein is indefatigable.

Now an early dinner awaits him. This evening he conducts the Philharmonic. After the concert he will greet the dignitaries, the friends and acquaintances, and, outside, the fans waiting to see him in the Green Room and at the stage entrance of Philharmonic Hall. Later he will go out with friends or simply come home. Later still, back in his study, he will begin working on the scores he will conduct on his next Philharmonic program. A typical day will thus have come to an end. Another like it will begin the following morning.

Leonard Bernstein has kept to this sort of schedule for years. I speculate on how he will manage once he leaves the Philharmonic. Actually, he loves the tempo and dynamics of racing against time. It is a fulfilling, even a necessary kind of race for Lenny. In a way, it takes him away from himself—from depression, from dissatisfaction, from frustration. And it takes him away from despair. As we sit and talk, as it again grows very late, Bernstein seems indeed a man of enormous contradictions. He is pulled and torn by so many forces. The wish to be the inward man—the composer, the writer, the thinker. The need to be the public figure—the conductor, the teacher, the celebrity.

"What is it like, living with yourself?" I finally ask him. "What kind of feelings go through you? Have you found a key to yourself?"

"I have long since given up trying to find a key to myself philosophically because one lives in a world of despair," he answers. "It is impossible to find a key in the old Spinoza or Kant kind of systems, which are based on the proofs of the existence of God, and a supreme intelligence that 'must have an ultimate purpose.'

"I feel that only out of habit in a way, because it has long been my habit to feel that kind of optimistic philosophy. I have never really been able to fall into the existential pattern of our time with any ease. It's partly my upbringing and the deep contact I made with Judaism in my young years, and partly a naturally optimistic nature, I guess. I'm told that. But when in my despair I examine any kind of philosophical system that can give me hope, or explain anything to me, or explain myself to me, or my relation to the world or to life or to art, or can explain the function or necessity of my art and its relation to existence,

I am absolutely stuck." And Leonard Bernstein smiles—a sad smile, really, a smile that is also a question.

So, at fifty, Leonard Bernstein confronts the reshaping of his world, both private and public. Seated here at his desk, he looks at me and says, "By mid-1969 I will be free of the Philharmonic as music director. Then I will be flexible again, which means going back to that old haphazard way of living, I suppose. Except that by then I will have learned to control it a bit more. Although I'm already in trouble about offers. It's not just the offers. It's the ones one *wants* to accept that present the problems."

Leonard Bernstein at fifty: a man of vast complexity and staggering accomplishment. Lenny, who at twenty-five became the youngest, most volatile, most publicized all-around musician America has ever produced, has emerged as Bernstein, a major international figure whose place in the world of conducting is assured, and whose stature as a front-ranking twentieth-century man of music is unquestioned.

As for the inner man? A sentence from *The Memoirs of Hadrian*, which Bernstein read to me in Ansedonia, is as good a nonsummation as any: "When I seek deep within me for knowledge of myself, what I find is obscure, internal, unformulated and as secret as any complicity."